HUNGRY THINGS

NORMAN HENDRICKS

SEVERED PRESS
HOBART TASMANIA

HUNGRY THINGS

ISBN: 978-1-925711-87-5

ONE

Jacob Eichkoff had been the count man for Yani the Yid, toughest numbers runner in Astoria. Now Jake was an old man, and he was being stalked by something, some animal in the weeds.

Jake had known some crappy people, some that scared him, but no one ever saw Ike the Kike sweat. He was the one who threw scares into other players. If Yani said Jake had to do collections, he did collections, and he never came back short, regardless of the cost to knees or old ladies' noses. Jake ran with a rough crowd once. Now, he looked around the dump he had been shipped off to and thought: *What a shit hole.* The sound of rustling issuing from a growth of palmetto surrounding the golf course only made it clearer, the salad days had wilted. What was it? Rats? Gators?

There were no Darren Minor songs about killer gators.

Darren Minor was a notable rock star of the 1970's, known for his soft blue eyes and watery chords, backing syrupy lyrics about long sunsets and tropical mixed drinks, best enjoyed after an eightball of coke. Minor had a major following throughout the world who lapped up everything Darren; from new musical releases to signature Banana Republic plantation hats, sportswear for the more active disciples to resorts co-owned by Minor in various small cities dotting the Gulf of Mexico. That's where Jake (Ike-the-Kike to his friends) lived now, the Gulf coast of Florida. But it wasn't any resort.

The rustling increased. What was hiding in the weeds and how many were there?

"Better scoot, if you know what's good for ya!"

The aging rocker-turned-entrepreneur's latest endeavour was retirement homes catering specially to longtime fans of the Mine-man, a group who self-identified as Daq-heads because of the multiple Minor songs in major keys referring to daiquiris. Jacob lived in one of these places, Minor Mansions, on a back street of Dunedin, Florida, about a mile from the causeway leading out to Clearwater and the Gulf. Jacob was no Daq-head but here he was all the same, and he hated it.

The rustling sounded urgent and slippery, like some long body rubbing past a scratching post.

What a shit hole.

Eileen, the late Mrs. Eichkoff, had been a daq-head, blood of rum, and had died the first month they moved into the Mansions, leaving Jacob there with some hundred other old people waiting to die to the accompaniment of soft, instrumental versions of Minor's top hits, all twelve of them, and only them.

Jacob liked golf. He was not that great at it, but he considered it a worthy distraction. Minor Mansions promised a full eighteen-hole golf course, but that turned out to be mini golf. The adult golf course was two holes of treacherous par three ball searching. The region was out back of the apartment buildings, near the huge drainage culvert where Jacob had learned to keep an eye out for gators. The second of the two holes came particularly close to the wet super-ditch, barely discernable from the overgrowth of palmetto choking the pitiful course.

How it was possible to lose a ball on a two-hole course, Jacob could not say, but his second Titleist just bounced off the so-called green (turf over concrete), past a sentry of palmetto, and into the long sawgrass beyond.

He was in no mood. "Fuck."

It was a Tuesday, that meant brownies were put out on the breakfast bar. John fucking Feingold took the brownie right off Jacob's plate when the old golfer got up to go to the pisser.

So when the palmetto fronds went all jazz hands and some animal grunted with rumbling anger from the sawgrass, Jacob thought that was just perfect. He pictured a gator the size of a sheep dog squatting protectively over his Titleist like it was one of its eggs. It was really not worth it, a stupid ball, but that's not how Jacob was playing it today. He really looked forward to his brownie! Damn Feingold.

"Hey! Jurassic Park!" He yelled unconvincingly at the wild growth invading the second hole. "I'm giving you one chance, motherfucker!"

Jacob was a quiet man and his voice sounded like the tremulous whistle of an old innertube. He was once the terror of Red Hook. No crew of his would dare unload a freighter in anything more than a single morning, unless he told them to, and God save the shoreman that defied Ike-the-Kike Eichkoff. Now, he felt all his power gone. Even a stupid reptile was not afraid. Getting old sucked.

Fuck it. He pulled his seven iron (the broadsword of clubs) from his fancy push bag and waded into the palmetto. He could instantly see the dark figure skulking in the brown sawgrass, the lip of the drainage culvert a cracked horizon beyond the oily black of the creature.

"Come on, get out of there!" Jacob said. "I still got a shot at par, slime bag."

He punctuated his assessment of today's round with a parry of his seven iron at a clump of grass.

More angry murmuring, something like a growl, and a sickly slurp like water backing up in a laundry drain.

"Hey…"

It was then that Jacob realized the thing in the sawgrass was no gator. Though dark--black as midnight really--and slimy, the thing slithered through the grass.

Everyone in Florida knew about the pythons. If you own a home and own a pet, you know you can't let Fido or Fluffy loose without supervision for fear of a goliath Burmese python slipping a ton of snake muscle around your sweet packet of love and squeezing it into a snake meal pellet.

Jacob wasn't worried. Pythons were slow and preferred hiding in the bushes, staying out of trouble, even the ones pushing a ton.

"Go back to Myanmar and give me back my--"

But this thing wasn't slow and it didn't back down. On the contrary, it slipped forward. The first thing Jacob thought was that it was some other damnable snake, like a cobra.

We got those? He had time to think. He would not be surprised.

Whatever it was it launched out of the tall grass and locked onto Jacob's ankle. It sank neatly into the knee high tube socks he wore to cover the embolism hose he sported day and night and thought nobody knew about.

There was no ripping. It was as though neither sock nor skin was there to slow it down. Blood eased through the white socks just as Jacob had a moment of clarity.

"It that a fucking eel?"

TWO

He was a Daq-head, no doubt, but even Dan Nickle could use a break. That's why he was sitting at the tin patio table to escape the perpetual pumping of the soft versions of the Darren Minor tunes. He watched the sun dropping into the Gulf and the mysterious, giant trucks rolling into the unmarked depot across the road, Minor Mansion's only neighbor.

The chain link fence rolled open. The big trucks rolled in. The fence closed. Not even a security guard to proctor the departures and arrivals.

This is what he was thinking when someone tapped on his shoulder.

"That's not prescribed Minor gear," a familiar, feminine voice said. "You'll forfeit your jello. A black polo tee? Where's the Hawaiian floral or the Banana Republic safari hat?"

Dan turned, not too quickly, and smiled up at Sue.

"I left them in Paradise," he said, looking back to the complex across the street and the high fence fortressing it against the likes of Dan, denizen of a novelty themed old age home. "What do you suppose really goes on over there?"

Sue sat down across the tin table from Dan, wiping rotted guava leaves from the chair and further wiping at the stains the leaves left behind. She wore white jogging pants.

Daring soul, Dan thought. His eyes slid over her pants, particular parts in sharp focus. He quietly chastised himself for such adolescent behavior. They were all past that now. Weren't they?

"I always thought it was something mundane, water treatment or lost button recovery," Sue said. When Dan looked over, she had a smirk.

He harrumphed, not unpleasantly, at her remark.

4

Sue kept her lipstick neat, Dan noted. Not many of the Daq-head gals seemed to be able to manage it, many abandoning make-up all together. Sue made the effort and Dan noticed.

A distant rumbling announced the approach of a large truck, clearly heading toward the subject of Dan's musings, the button recovery plant across the road.

The home was on a thin peninsula that jutted out into Pope Channel between Dunedin and Clearwater Beach, the water break that fended off the greater Gulf beyond. Minor Mansions and the mysterious plant were the only two buildings on the mangrove cluttered peninsula. No trucks came to the Mansions. Hardly anyone did.

It was a dump truck the size of a humpback whale. Sue covered her mouth with a handkerchief in anticipation of the dust cloud the monster vehicle's passage would kick up.

The goliath truck swung in as the fence opened automatically. An equally oversized black SUV trailed the dumper, and the fence closed. The curtains of dust settled. All very smooth and well timed.

The brittle lawn, grass too hard to lounge on, beiged as the road dust settled on the stiff blades.

"All rather mysterious," Dan said.

Sue nodded. "Oh!" she said. "Speaking of mysteries, Jacob Eichkhoff is in the infirmary, probably headed to the hospital."

"What do you say? Ike-the-Kike?" Dan said, holding a moment to wait for the slow shake of her head. Dan knew she did not like the moniker. It was no use explaining that was how Jake introduced himself. He got the disapproving shake from Sue, and smiled back at her, satisfied. "What's wrong with that grouch?"

She managed to reach across the table to give Dan's upper arm a playful flick. "That's just the thing. No one really seems to know, but there are murmurings in the pipes that he was attacked by something."

"A gator? He's on those pathetic golf holes out there by the culvert all the time. A battalion of the little monsters must come up out of there."

"I don't know," Sue said. "But, somehow, I don't think so."

Some old man response bubbled out of Dan. "Hmph."

"Listen," Sue said, "I'm volunteering over in the infirmary today, refilling rubber gloves and the such. You want to come give our old friend a visit?"

"Hmph," Dan said. "He's no friend of mine."

The next flick on his upper arm had a little more whip to it. "Oh! Come on! I want to see, and I want you to come."

"Geez," Dan said, "you'd think we were married."

"I should be so cursed."

Dan smiled and pushed himself creakily out of the aluminum patio chair.

***

If there is an easy way to do things, women can't remember it. But, Dan remembered, how women are; he'd married a couple of them. Volunteering in the infirmary came with a uniform. Its simplicity astounded Dan, just a pink frock cinched around the waist with a single white ribbon belt. Sue had disappeared for twenty minutes inside her suite to make this outfit 'change' happen.

Dan tried not to grouse. Friends had a way of drying up in the Mansions like a thin layer of Ben Gay on legs that had done seventy years of walking. Some legs in the place had worn out at least that much shoe leather.

"You haven't seen my uniform yet, have you?"

Dan shook his head. He had not completely cooled. Twenty minutes for a robe to be cinched?

"Do you like it?"

He eyed her. "You look stunning." He wasn't married to her. He had to remind himself; that helped.

The pictures people see on the virtual tour of Minor Mansions must have been taken in the infirmary, Dan figured. An atrium with high ceilings and sky lights, the airy medical facility seemed vast compared to the narrow hallways and cramped common rooms. The place was not a dump, but Dan sometimes wished he had the computer skills to hack the facility's website and offer a little more fact into the sales pitch.

Borrow from the truth, lend yourself to a lie…

It was one of *his* songs. *His* very words. The minor god.

Sue grabbed a cart of oral meds.

"You can give those out?" Dan asked.

She elbowed the old man. "No, they need refilling, get me?" She offered a wink. "And today, you're my assistant."

All rather hush-hush with a generous schmear of intrigue. If he was twenty, this would have been great fun for Dan.

"Nobody's here, like usual," he said. "Just like when I got that rash after traipsing through hedges looking for the official shuttlecock for the badminton tourney."

"The one we lost?"

"Exactly."

"You don't let go easily, do you?"

He chuckled. "Let's find Jacob."

They couldn't find him, and that was funny because the infirmary was an open circle. Herb Bunting lay on one bed, looking up at the ceiling, the neck brace keeping him from identifying them on their *investigation*. He looked rather untended to Dan, just as he had been when he had that awful rash, stripes going up his legs like whip lashes.

Sue peered under beds. "What the...?"

But a spinning scan on Dan's part revealed a facet of the infirmary not yet uncovered. What looked like a ginormous central support column was a little more than a load-bearing feature. There was a door.

"What's up with this?" Dan asked, jerking a thumb in the direction of the metal door with a single small, opaque glass window centering the top half of the portal like the eye of a cyclops. "See how it's not perfectly round all the way up, kind of spiraling a bit like..."

"A staircase. Let's try something." Sue stepped forward, and looking around like she was G. Gordon Liddy using a White House toilet, checked around before producing an ID card from the pocket of the long awaited frock. "Watch!"

Dan watched. Sue swiped. Nothing. There was a red light next to the swipe through. It stayed red.

"Hrmph."

"Save your noise," Sue said. It wasn't often Dan saw her mad. Somehow it tickled him. She swiped and swiped again. All red.

Sue considered for a moment. She spun and walked away. Dan shrugged and followed.

The nurse's station was just on the other side of the strange column and the stairs that hid within.

The bottom half of a saloon door disallowed them from entering the station. But, not long after, a dowager of sufficient glower appeared.

"I need the key for the upstairs," Sue told the scowling nurse. Dan knew he should know her name. "I have a refill for Eichkoff."

"No one goes up there."

And that seemed to be that. The matron turned, stoney faced, a period at the end of the sentence.

Sue tried to mince. "But, I…"

"No one," the matron said. "Mostly storage up there, but if a quarantine is necessary…"

It seemed to Dan the full-figured nurse felt no need to finish the idea.

"Quarantine?" Sue asked. "Why--"

But Dan really did not need to hear anymore. "Thanks!" he yelled to the matron, too used to the poor hearing of his fellow Daq-heads. "We're good." He dragged at Sue by the elbow.

"What?" Sue asked.

"You heard? Quarantine?"

Sue's eyes were like something alight, an oil fire on seawater. "Jacob is our friend."

"Jacob is an old crabby ass like most all the old dudes in here."

A soft sell instrumental version of *I Can Almost See Acapulco From Here*, Minor's third top ten hit of 1977, dripped down on them as Sue spun determinedly toward some destination Dan could not imagine.

"Whoa, what-the?"

But she was gone from the infirmary down one of the brightly painted, but choked, corridors deep into the belly of a side investment by a rock star whose career was built on the idea that everyone longs to sit at a tiki bar drinking themselves blind just before they swim out into the tepid depths of the Gulf of Mexico.

Dan followed his friend, his only friend, a girlfriend, of sorts. What were his options? Hang with Nurse Ratched?

He called out to Sue. "Hang on!"

She did not wait. Her sneakers were just that, silencers shooting down the tilework. They spotted Dr. Marko at the same time. He represented what the brochures called 'Attentive Medical Staff.'

Dan supposed the Doc tried. There were some hundred and twenty Daq-heads hole-up in the Mansions and only the one doc.

Sue did not even try to engage him. She just did what they called in Dan's old neighborhood the bump-and-run, and came away with Marko's ID.

Dan mouthed the words: "Are you nuts?"

But Sue did not answer nor waited for further protests. She hurried the ID to the infirmary and swiped it on the access panel for the secret stairs. Green, good to go.

Sue smiled and winked at Dan who was pretty sure he did not want to go up the stairs. But Sue did; she was gone.

"Hrmph."

But he followed, musing on whatever part of his gallantry was stored and wished he could cut it out.

Dan was sure there were lights, but they did not bother. He was also sure the central AC filling the facility (thank God) did not penetrate this passageway. A door of the same type capped the top.

Dan reached for Sue, suddenly sure he did not want to see. "Wait."

But she did not wait, and when she opened the door at the top, the smell that drifted down confirmed Dan's fears. Worse than that, something black and slippery slopped onto the top step, seemingly blocking their breaching the secret quarantine zone.

Sue was undaunted. But she should have been. The one slippery bit of black stickiness was just a meager spill off from the inches of horror coating the causeway surrounding the circular dome of the upper infirmary.

Sue pushed on but Dan grabbed her. "No!"

There was a Korean War; he'd missed it, but not mandatory service, and there were enough WWII vets around then to shame one into a basic sense of manhood. Dan knew danger, and he knew he could not let a woman walk into it.

He pushed past her and stepped onto the quarantined floor. There was no safe place to step. Black, squiggly commas littered the floor in a gel layer trailing back to a figure alone on a bed among boxes of records--now darkened with the siphoned wet soaking the floor.

Dan grew up in rural Massachusetts and a frog wallow was not something unknown to him. By late summer, after steamy nights of chirping song, the female frogs filled every collection of water--no matter how small--with eggs. No time to waste, the male frogs littered these pustules with their sperm and then the most disgusting of all--acres of bog alive with tadpoles. This is what happened to the secret quarantine zone and it all seemed to emanate from the figure on the lone bed--Jacob Eichkhoff, Ike-the-Kike, who was clearly dead, a mass of the squiggling figures pouring from under the soaked blankets covering what was, hopefully, his corpse.

Dan pushed Sue back down the stairs, deaf to protests.

A slick, squishing sound told Dan the yolk sac of squiggly worms had overrun the lip and was trickling down the stairs. He didn't want to, but he peeked. A shower of clear mucous chased them out of the dark, circular stairwell.

THREE

"I don't understand." It was the fifth time she said it, and, though Dan was pretty sick of hearing the statement, he could understand. "If it was as bad as you say, how can the staff hide it? Why hasn't an ambulance taken Jake away? It can't be as bad as you said. Maybe I should see."

Dan had taken Sue to the solarium, brightly painted but choked with planted palmetto and ferns. She tried to get up from the overstuffed armchair. He gently pushed her back down. He told himself it was for her own good, but it was *his* hand that was shaking.

"Nothing doing, darlin'," he said. "Whatever was happening up there is bad, very bad, and dangerous. What you're going to see next is not an ambulance, but men in hazmat suits."

A vehicle rolled by outside and Dan whipped around to try to peer through the glass portions of the front door, the main entrance to the lobby. A big truck rolled into the mysterious facility across the road, the missing button factory.

He noted one of the many pockets of his off-white cargo shorts was missing a button. Dan thought perhaps he should cross the street, drag a four-iron across the fence, and demand his button. Then he knew he was not thinking straight. There had never been a problem with his heart, but he instinctively put a hand to his chest anyway.

"Dan," Sue said, "we have to do something. Maybe they don't know."

"Oh, they know. How can they not? I mean…"

The front doorbell rang. There was no reason for it; one could see into the lobby through the crystal settings around the door, but there was a bell. It was strange to hear and it made Dan cringe. He got up from his own overstuffed chair.

Sue grabbed one of his specked hands and used it to pull herself to her feet. "What is it?"

"No one uses the bell."

Others must have noted the same strangeness, for a cavalcade of seniors in Hawaiian shirts and Bermuda shorts ambled into the lobby.

The doorbell chimed again. It was not a bad sound, just an electric, pre-programmed bell tone, but it gave Dan the chills. None of the residents moved any closer to the door, and when Maria, the receptionist, returned to the front desk, the bell chimed again, chilling Dan to the bone.

This is it, he thought, *it's all different from this moment.*

He said as much aloud.

He discovered Sue had never let go of his hand, gripping it tightly now. "What do you mean? What is it?"

"Just a feeling," he said.

"Isn't anyone going to get that?" Maria asked. "What's got into your shorts today? I don't have a PHD in hospitality, you know. You can answer the door too."

She stepped from behind the hotel front desk-style reception area and moved toward the front entrance of Minor Mansions. Dan almost cried out to stop her.

The clack of her heels on the sandstone tiles preceded Maria's quick reach for the saloon handles. She whipped open the door.

And sure enough there they were. Men in hazmats suits.

***

All the special lenses reserved for looking at smartphone screens appeared from pockets of robes, cargo shorts, and sewing bags. Between them, the residents of the Mansions must have three-thousand years of experience, Dan figured, but they only trusted the elongated pill boxes to tell them the truth. After all, their kids gifted them the phones. Heck, they could even do a video thing with the grandkids. It was almost as good as being there. And who would want to be there, with the grandchildren, when you could be here, under the slow morphine drip of Musak twists of Darren Minor tunes? Maybe the answer was in the smartphones they held under magnifying lenses as if the old crones were trying to set them on fire.

And, Dan supposed, he could not blame them. Who knew FEMA's disaster levels and associated quarantine actions?

Gilbert Echevia did, but no one listened to the facility's loud mouth and know-it-all.

"Dan," Gilbert said. He saw Dan, sitting facing away from him, sipping at a bottle of water and trying to ignore the clatter of the gurney coming through the front entrance, presumably to drag Jake Eichkoff out of the place. Somehow, Dan had not noticed, but once he heard Gilbert's voice, his stomach dropped. "I asked the man, I asked him. You know what he told me?"

"No, Gil."

"We got a level one contain and coordinate; that's what we got."

It's probably what all the other daq-heads were pumping into their phones right now: *contain and coordinate.*

"But Dan, Dan, let me tell you something, the really weird thing."

Do you have to?

"Dan I think these guys aren't FEMA or CDC at all…"

Now Dan was paying attention. "What makes you say that?"

"I'll tell you, my friend," Gil said, locked onto his audience. "And this is not shit, I used to work for a cleaning crew, no shit. Everything from post weddings to murder scene stuff. And what these guys are toting, what they're wearing, it's the same stuff I wore. Those suits have about the same biohazard protection as cutting a bra in half and strapping it to your kisser. Follow?"

Dan was not sure he wanted to, but something rang true, rang like the front bell.

No one rings the front bell. It rang false.

Dan leaned in to hear more when he felt a soft hand on his shoulder.

"Talk to you?" It was Sue. Part of Dan was relieved. But was Gil onto something?

It was all damn strange. Everyone felt it, looking into the crystal screens for guidance.

Gil reached out, reluctant to lose a disciple. "You know it's like Darren's song."

Dan was already out of the conversation but turned to at the mention of The Master. "Huh?"

"'You gotta know some to grow some, ain't no better teacher than the ripples on the water.' You gotta believe that, don't ya?"

"Sure."

Dan let Sue direct him away.

Some random daq-head tried to flag them as they passed. "Hey! What's this *Bing*? What happened to *Google*? Can you help me?"

"What makes him think we can help?" Dan asked.

Sue patted his arm. "We're ambulatory."

And they kept ambling, out the common area surrounding reception and the front lobby, past the atrium, heading generally toward the game room. It was empty except during tourney time. A whole crowd of five old daq-heads would jam in around the pool tables while another oldster in Bermuda shorts would peer through thick lenses at the dart board. It was empty now, though.

Sue spun on him. "Dan, something's wrong here."

"You're telling me? Ike the Kike just exploded into a river of worms."

"Please don't call him that," Sue said, then glancing over Don's shoulder. "How did FEMA find out about it so soon?"

"So soon? How do we know Jake hasn't been leaking those things for days?"

Sue shook her head, her dangly earrings jostling so that they clinked. "No," she said. "I talked to Laura, the Activities Director, she's an RN you know, and she was telling me the doctor wasn't working the Mansions the day Jake came back from the course complaining of what he said was a snake bite."

"And?"

Sue tapped him meaningfully on the chest with a fake nail. "She told me only the doctor can make the determination to call FEMA."

Dan walked to the entryway from the hall into the game room. He peered down toward the lobby. Guys in hazmats were progressing to and fro from the general direction of the infirmary, but suddenly, to Dan, their protective gear didn't appear all that resistant.

Dan thought of the trucks going into the facility across the road.

"Sir?" It was a strange voice, one muffled by air filters. Dan found himself back on his heels, a face glaring at him through the visor of a hazmat. "Sir? And Ma'mn? Would you come with me?"

Sue took a noticeable step back. "Us? But what did we…"

"Please, ma'am. My commander wants to speak with you two."

Dan noted the defensiveness rising within him and the shift to indignation. "What do you want with us? We didn't do anything. We're not ill, or symptomatic, so FEMA or the CDC has nothing to do with us." But it was really some sort of unnamed terror that squirmed, like a river of black worms in his gut, and the helplessness of being faced with a tall, young man in antibacterial armor. Dan remembered he was the old dotter who had to call on his roommate, Kirk, to help him tie his shoelace, before finally relenting to the idea he'd get Velcro.

"Young man--"

"Please sir, you two were the ones to come on Mr. Eichkoff in his current state?"

Sue stepped forward and clenched at Dan. "How'd you know?"

"Ma'am, please?"

Dan nodded, helplessly. They followed the unidentifiable FEMA official down the hallway away from the abandoned billiards and ping-pong tables.

***

"Swear to Christ." The huge man encased in tactical wear sat across the desk normally belonging to the facility's director. "This must be one of those white folk things."

He leaned back heavily in the chair that was not his, his enormous size seeming, to Dan, to threaten the elasticity of the chair's back support.

His smile was wide and warm, but his dark eyes did not seem to have any mirth. "I mean, come on," he said, "I'm a big Public Enemy fan, the biggest, but if they opened a facility called The Terror Dome, I wouldn't likely pop on my big clock and settle in to spend my final chapter there."

Dan said nothing.

"Darren Minor? Please. What was it on the brochure that got you to commit your final years here? Shuffleboard courts with parrots instead of numbers? The big mural of dolphins at sunset over the handball court?"

He was big and he was black and he was just official enough to send a shiver down Dan's back.

"But really," Dan started. "What is this all about?"

Sue, who silently hugged her arms around the chest of her bright athletic wear, came alive for a moment. "We didn't do anything."

It was half-petulant child and half-old crank, and it made Dan smile. "Is this what FEMA does?" he said, defending his friend. "Harassing grandmothers?"

This seemed to poke a hole in the commander's aggressiveness.

"Well, grandma, you got some skills," the commander said. "We wasted a good peck of time accessing the upstairs storage area Doc Marko was using as an emergency quarantine area. He could not find his card, but Doc is no dummy. He recalled the bump-and-run grandma here pulled."

"My name is Susan, once Susan Mayfield, mister…"

"You can call me The Major, Mrs. Mayfield, and I'm sorry if I've come across a little gruff but we have a real situation here, and I'm on the clock with a hard deadline, emphasis on *dead*."

The Major, huh?

It was then that Dan noted the identity patch above the black man's left breast. It was covered with a length of duct tape. The agent that brought them to the annexed office was still in his hazmat suit, standing like a cigar store Indian in the corner. Then it clicked for Dan--the suits aren't protecting them from what's upstairs; it's to conceal their identity.

The Mansions never seemed so far away and isolated from the rest of the world. For some odd reason, Dan wondered if he'd ever see his family again. It had been his idea to come here, but there hadn't been any protests. He had a daughter and a son and seven grandchildren, and he was at the end of a peninsula jutting out into Pope Channel with a bunch of old, feeble devotees to a musician whose music is most likely encountered when pumping some quarters into a diner jukebox.

Dan had become a grump. He was a million miles from anywhere he ever called home. Despite Sue's best efforts, he grew a little more crotchety every day. But he was not a hard man, he was just scared. Growing more scared as his old life drifted into the past. Now, even this life was lost to the clean up crew from Hades.

Dan began to cry.

"Hey!" the Major said, standing.

Sue put out a hand. "Oh, Danny."

"Hey, old timer," the Major said, his tone softening. He brought his great girth (top heavy with linebacker shoulders) to get face-to-face with Dan. "Hold on there. You're not in any kind of trouble here." The Major snuck a peek at his compatriot in the corner. "At least no more trouble than the rest of us. But if we're going to save the day here, I need your help but quick. Do you think you can help me, Danny?"

Dan sniffed. "Dan, just Dan."

"Well, Dan," the Major said. "Do you think you can help me, sir? We all need your help on this one, Dan."

Dan nodded, snatching a tissue off the absent director's desk.

"What, exactly, is going on here, Major?" Sue asked.

"Well, Sue, that's a little hard to say, exactly, but you two seem to have it a little more on the ball than the other dead-heads around here."

"Daq-heads," Dan said. "Darren Minor fans are called daq-heads   cause--"

"Never mind about that, Dan," the Major said, holding back a certain level of frustration. "But let's just say I deputize you two and then you can do a couple of things for me."

"Sure," Dan said. "But the staff here is a lot younger and more able I would think--"

"By getting upstairs, you two have shown more resourcefulness than any of the folks being paid to be here. I bet both of you have had far more experience than the doctors or nurses. Plus, they are needed *here*. I need you to take a little trip with me."

Sue clutched a loose pleat in her fancy sweatpants. "A trip?"

"Like I said, I need two things, folks." The Major stood and signaled the agent in the corner who left the office without a word. "Tell me about what you saw upstairs and give me a little tour of your golf course."

"That'll be a short trip," Dan said, sniffing and smiling at Sue, who laughed.

FOUR

"This is it?" the Major asked, hands on broad hips. "How much do you daq-heads pay to be here?"

They had been joined by a small squad of faceless, hazmatted agents. Dan and Sue had led the men to the two-hole course, a part of the property not visible from the road.

"No sand traps or water hazards?" the Major asked.

"There's plenty of hazards, no doubt," Dan said. They were standing on the walkway between hole number one and tee number two. Dan started walking, pointing and leading to the wall of palmetto where the fairway for the second hole took a sharp bend. "Tough avoiding the wilds there, next to impossible if the breeze kicks up from the bay. Right behind there is a gulley topped with cement; it's the drainage outlet for the Minor Mansions property. If Jake ran into trouble, he likely found it chasing a ball into that mess."

The group marched up to the edge of the fairway (no real rough on the course) and peered past the palmetto fronds to the sawgrass beyond.

"There's a drop-off just beyond the grass," Dan said.

Major kept his eyes on the tall sawgrass as he spoke. "Mrs. Mayfield? Will you do me a favor?"

"Uh, yes."

"Stay here." The Major stepped through fanned palmetto fronds without looking back.

Dan shrugged and followed.

Sue called after them. "By myself?"

The Major barked at the sultry air. "Brenner!"

One of the men sweltering inside a hazmat stepped back onto the fairway.

"She's not going to be happy," Dan said.

"I get that," the Major returned, pushing past palmetto, reaching for each other like batwing doors of a saloon. "You two aren't a couple?"

"No, sir."

"Then we won't own her feelings, will we?"

"I suppose not."

Major stopped short at the sawgrass. The sun was powerful. The Major took off his soft-billed cap and wiped at his forehead. Dan felt fine about it; he'd come a long way and lived a long life in the cold to earn the comforting bake of a sun running its daily route toward The Gulf. None of the men hiding in the hazmats looked the least bit wobbly, though Dan felt claustrophobic looking at them.

The major considered the grass. "Hmm," he grumbled. "Could be a whole lot of trouble hiding in there."

An electric hum preceded an address from a hazmat. "Rig it to burn, sir?"

"Not in the dry season, Bilford," the Major replied. "No need to chuck the baby with the bathwater at this point. Not until we can determine that containment is not an option."

Not an option? Dan thought. *Contain what?*

"Gentlemen," the Major barked. "Sticks!"

As one, the hazmats unzipped secret pockets in their protective gear. Once free of the pockets, the foot-long sticks whipped out, unleashing several hinges connecting additional lengths, each segment successively longer and thinner.

"Y'all expecting to go blind, or something?" Dan asked.

The Major lifted a finger in the air and held it there. "You've heard of beating the bushes?" the Major asked. He did not wait for an answer. "Forward gentlemen."

The sticks cut the air, producing sharp whistles.

"You think he was bitten by a lion?" Dan asked.

The Major did not respond. The hazmats moved slowly through the grass, beating the air.

Dan's blood froze when one of the men stopped and called for the Major. The big black man waded into the waist-high grass, tall enough to hide a puma or the Vietcong. Dan really hated what The Major did next. "Come on, Dan."

To hell with that. He thought he said it aloud, but apparently not because he too waded in. Each tickle of sawgrass against Dan's bare knees seemed alive with ticks or scorpions. Hazmat protection would be right nice about now. Even The Major's paramilitary gear with boots halfway up the calf would be great.

Dan eased up next to the hazmats, putting two of them between himself and whatever was waiting to be discovered.

An area roughly the size of a fallen man had been beaten into the grass, flattening the blades in a sun-browned radial pattern.

"Probably where they found Eichkoff, sir," one of the hazmats reported.

Major nodded. "And, as our friend Dan here indicated, we should follow from this point to the gulley."

Hazmat pointed. "And there's this, Sir."

Dan shifted from foot-to-foot, trying to get a peek at the thing he really didn't want to see. At the center of the hurricane of reeds, an eye of sticky black oozed into the dry loam, turning to a septic mud. It smelled of sea salt and dog farts.

Dan pulled back. "What is that?"

The Major did not respond to Dan. "We have our sign, gentlemen," he said. "I think we know where we're going."

Dan didn't, and when the men pushed forward into tall grass, he remained. They disappeared from view around an elbow of palmetto. In a moment, Dan knew, they'd be over the edge into the culvert, chasing whatever it was they thought they'd found, and he was left behind, with the sticky spot.

He had no reason to follow into the long grass, full of other geysers of ick and into who-knows-what, but otherwise he was left holding his dick or crawling back out onto the fairway to be with Sue. In other words, with the rest of the women.

Dan sighed deeply and followed into the palmetto.

When he got to the edge of the culvert, he saw a short rappelling system had been established. The Major stood above his men, the only agent yet to spill down the embankment to the cement scoop below.

"Oh," the Major said, spying Dan. "Decided to join us, Mr. Nickle? A man your age must have served your country at one point, eh? Well, grab hold and take the quick drop, less than ten feet. Just for efficiency, really."

And he was gone. Dan looked down, holding his dick.

Instead of rapelling (something Dan had practiced as an eighteen-year-old in the service), he grabbed the length of cord and used it to stabilize himself as he attempted to skirt the drop off and skitter down the grass-clogged embankment. Ultimately, this bit of daring proved too much for feet that weren't used to--and probably not capable of--much more than working a two-hole golf course or quick strolls around the mangrove and palmetto choked property.

A tangle of sawgrass reminded him he was no Fred Astaire, and over he went; if his grip on the cord hadn't tightened automatically, he would have gone ass-over-polo shirt, probably cracking his neck. As it was, he swung down like a fossilized Tarzan, spinning out of control until a hazmat glove reached out and steadied him. He was pulled to the ground, his heart beating a Buddy Shore tattoo, his hands missing several layers of skin.

The hands hurt immediately.

"Glad to have you, Sir," the Hazmat said through his air filter.

The Major was not laughing but the amusement he mixed into his game face like water with some scotch was noticeable to Dan, who blew on his hands. Old skin is delicate, and he was missing a bunch.

The relatively flat area of the concrete they occupied stood before the gaping mouth of the drainage pipe, a black pupil in the beige iris, surrounded by lashes of palmetto green.

"Gentlemen," the Major barked. "Weapons hot!"

Dan saw M-16s but a closer look revealed that the agents produced a phalanx of light arms the likes of which Dan had never seen, except maybe in sci fi war movies of the *not too distant future*.

Not much bigger around than the bush beaters they had unfolded from discrete, lengthy pockets in the hazmat suits, where these guns came from, Dan could not say. They were as delicate as starships made of Legos and as intimidating as slender howitzers. They held them out toward the dark, yawning mouth of the drain pipe.

22

Dan hesitated, but he felt like he was a step behind in the script for this scene. "What, exactly are you guys expecting to come rolling out of there, The Creature From the Black Lagoon?"

There was no response to this, and Dan had to wonder if he should have gone back to the golf course.

Then something sticky happened. A slurp followed by a wet pop introduced a small figure at the bottom swell of the drainage pipe. Half in the shadowy depths of the pipe, it lay in the weak stream trickling down the center of the culvert. It was the head of something.

A fish?

Or just its head, a long head, gulping for air but not flopping around in any great distress.

I was just kidding about the gillman from that stupid old movie, Dan thought.

It slipped forward in the tepid flow. It slid down the chute toward the marshy end of the culvert, on its way to the bay if a heavy military boot did not come down on its seemingly endless, neckless head.

The Major got it.

"Yep," said the Major, one boot on his trophy, "the New Zealand long finned eel."

Dan wasn't sure about the fins, but the thing was long, more than a yard of pure black. But, it was somehow reminiscent of the squiggly infestation in the quarantine area of Minor Mansions that had brought them to this point. In fact, the thing on the ground really only bore a passing resemblance to an eel, a really big eel.

"The long finned eel, during the mating season, will cross over miles of dry land to get to breeding grounds, then re-cross the same land-bridge to lay eggs in other waterways," the Major said. "And, it can be a really nasty character. This is probably what bit your friend."

Dan, unlike most of the other denizens of The Mansions only wore reading glasses for close up, some pretty honking big ones, but his distance vision was just fine; yet he wished he had them now because he just couldn't get a fix on what he was looking at.

Also, with the threat revealed as no real threat, the agents had not put away their weapons. They didn't even lower them.

Just as Dan was about to deny the identity of the slippery thing below the Major's boot, another wet *plop* echoed from inside the pipe. Then another. Like popcorn kernels thrown on an open fire, a rapid series of squishy reports issued from the opening.

Dan still a step behind, was somehow totally shocked when the Major raised his hand, made a pistol barrel with his forefinger and ring finger and leveled them in the direction of the black, wet maw of the pipe.

"Fire!"

The big boot held the eel. The Major shot it with his sidearm, a formidable forty-five.

They came out in great waves even as the first strafe of ordinance leapt into the breach. It was a fire fight like Dan had never seen or imagined.

It was as if the shadows inherent to the tunnel came to life. Waves of wriggling black roiled out of the hole, sickly, squirming balls of living pubic knots rolling toward them as though the earth was a cat coughing up a hairball of supposed eels.

BeeBeeBeeBeeBeeBeeBeeBeeBee!

The men fired into the mass, holding an even line. Dan hid behind The Major and clung to his back.

The reports from the weapons-of-the-near-future were high and piercing, sounding more like the screech of brakes on a subway car than rifles. Blue tracers cut into the pubic Indiana Jones ball, diminishing it some, but not enough to put Dan's mind at ease. His right foot sought purchase on the Major's oaken leg in preparation for climbing the man while his left foot turned to flee. In the end, he settled with screaming.

The ball roiled and turned and the blue tracers cut them down, the ball diminishing but not stopping.

"I don't think those are eels!" Dan screamed. The Major turreted his head and looked sideways in Dan's direction but did not lower his imposing sidearm. Dan was grateful he did not.

The men did not give ground. The ball was little more than a yard away.

BeeBeeBeeBeeBeeBee!

What the hell were those things? Why the hell weren't they all running away?

Please, God, please. I'll even devote myself, entirely, to the daiquiri smoothie dogma of Darren Minor as a film score for a life well lived.

"I hate Darren Minor!"

The Major laughed at Dan's pronouncement.

Just as they were about to be subsumed, the men stepped aside, the Major carrying Dan to the side like a senescent papoose.

The ball unfolded and collapsed, black squiggles slipping through and past the line of large men and their screeching weapons. The earsplitting cry of the weapons did not cease. The flood of squirming blackness flowed past the paramilitary assault squad like a Rorschach test come to life.

Ahhhhh! Dan screamed, not sure if the sound escaped his head.

The squishing torrent of unreality slipped past them, but only a few.

And, when the numbers of eels had reduced sufficiently for individual eradication, the agents kept firing. Stragglers paid the price. The agents followed stragglers down the culvert.

Where, Dan thought, *they'll be free, all the way from the bay and into The Gulf.*

The agents must have thought the same thing because they were meticulous in first thinning the herd, and then picking off cast-offs. The weird weapons screeched the eel-things to death. The unit slowly followed the flow of the shrinking mass of slurping creatures as they otherwise quietly slipped down the culvert toward a brief wetland that buffered the bay, now visible beyond.

The Major, in no particular hurry, followed his agents toward the bay. "No water for these suckers, gentlemen," he said.

The agents redoubled their efforts, eels exploding--with relatively sticky quiet--into small fountains of icor. Dan did not follow. He thought of scaling back up the embankment, but found his hands trembled. The culvert bent a bit, the men with the guns ambling out of Dan's field of vision. He had no drive to go, but he thought he heard something in the black tunnel at his back. He followed the guns.

"Hey!" But they did not wait. Luckily they were not going too fast. Good thing, his knees were a bit weak.

Dan turned the corner in time to see the men quicken their pace in order to cut off the swarm from making their way to the swampy stream. The culvert was blackened with the stuff that used to be inside the eel-things.

"Get 'em!" the Major barked.

A few of the remainders slipped down to the rubber-booted feet of the agents and seemed like they might get loose.

"Gentlemen!"

They doubled down with the weapons. Misses did not ricochet but pulverized cleanly on the cement. It was, it seemed to Dan, as though these guns were specifically designed to kill these giant, black worms.

Dan held his breath as the last eel danced and slipped, a serpentine ballerina about to execute a last jeté into the wet freedom it sought. Frustrated with missing the elusive shot, an agent jumped forward and brought his boot down on the thing, slowly grinding it into the cement, etching a tangle of sticky swirls worthy of being hung on a wall and called a decent Pollack rip off. The Major finished it with a shot from his forty-five, kicking up a sliver of cement from below the demolished creature.

Dan sighed. The Major turned and smiled.

"Situation contained," he said. He looked down at Dan. "Dan, my friend, we need to get you home in short order, I think."

Dan smiled. "Yes," he said, but then processed the slim urgency in the Major. "Is there a hurry. More eels?"

"No," the Major said, producing a thick cigar from a pocket in his fatigues. He poked the cigar at Dan's lower half. "You are in dire need of a change of clothes, Mr. Nickle."

Eel splash? Maybe a little, but he saw instantly what the concern was; he had peed his shorts.

FIVE

Dan untucked the short-sleeved collared shirt and pulled down the tails as low as possible to cover the crotch stain. They were approaching the golf course and he did not want Sue to see.

Sue didn't seem to notice Dan's shorts, but he must have looked off. "What happened? It sounded like someone was squeaking the world's largest balloon. Are you okay?"

The Major did not give Dan a chance to respond. "All set now, Mrs. Mayfield."

"It's Ms. Mayfield. My husband's name was March."

"Message received, Ms. Mayfield."

Dan passed Sue without stopping, pulling his Nokia from his shorts pocket.

Sue chased after. The agents barely had to stroll to keep up with the older pair's fastest gait. "Dan? What happened, Dan?"

He had his phone to his ear, not looking at Sue. "I'm calling my kids," he said, trying to keep it together. "That's it; I'm getting out of here."

Sue, starting to fall behind, put a hand on Dan's arm. "Daniel--"

"No!" he yelled. "I don't even really like Darren Minor! Why won't this thing work?' He shook the phone like he was trying to strangle a poisonous snake.

"All communications jammed," the Major said between puffs on his cigar. "Standard initial quarantine procedure for a cordon and contain."

Dan thought of all those old eyes peering myopically through the smear of their thick lenses at the pocket devices hardly any of them knew how to use but were glad, all the same, to receive something from their kids, anything from their kids.

"I bet they're all still looking at those things and wondering when it will tell them what's happening or when they'll see their families again," Dan said.

He heard the Major's voice from behind. "What?"

"Dan, whatever it is, it will be okay," Sue said.

They left the short golf course, spanned the unused shuffleboard courts, and reentered Minor Mansions.

From somewhere just off the main lobby, Dan caught Gilbert Enchevia's voice calling out from the hordes of gray wanderers. "Hey, Dan!" he called. "What's up with your shorts?'

He may have not been able to call on it, but Dan thought of a use for the phone that would break through this charade. He set his Nokia to take pictures and then placed it in one of his top front pockets with his hand on it, at the ready. It would have to be his turn for subterfuge in order to pull this one off. He hoped something would come to him as he walked back toward the infirmary.

They seemed ready, to be expecting those things, Dan thought, *even down to those weapons.*

The sound of that first, sticky thing dropping its black length on the culvert cement would haunt Dan to his grave, hopefully not hasten him to it. But those agents, again, did not freak out; it was more of a confirmation. They'd found what they were looking for. How eels from New Zealand supposedly related to that squirmy infestation that came pouring out of Ike would be an interesting tale to hear. It would also be pure bullshit.

Yes, Dan thought. T*hese guys are after something in particular.*

He had a few minutes. He had rushed off and why not? He'd peed his shorts. A change was in order.

They had expected that thing and all its squishiness.

The awful tadpole thing seeping from the man he called Jake had sounded squishy as they oozed across the floor, toward them, almost pursuing them.

Could that be a tell-tale sign? Squishy sound? The same noise as stepping on a soaked rug.

This caused Dan to stop in his stride, just about to pass the rec room, and take a step back. The recreation room had wall-to-wall carpet, thin industrial type typical of hallways connecting offices of an accounting firm. One of the few spaces that was not burning with forced brightness of a near tropic sun or UV-band strobes. This room, perhaps trying to recapture the intimate glow of a tavern backroom, had relatively dim mood lighting on long racks screwed into the ceiling, lighting the pool table, ping pong table, Golden Girls pinball game, and one fire extinguisher, the kind with the long rubber hose.

The rec room was also the only room without a window. A ceiling fan moved the central AC about. Dan fingered the spin knob controlling the fan, turning it down to a full stop. He could, while kneeling painfully on the edge of a pool table (all the natural padding lost from his knees and shins around the time some president Bush's lips said No New Taxes!), reach up and balance a billiard ball on the cylinder from which the wooden fan blades extended. He added four more balls, balancing them precipitously around the edges of the unmoving spoke.

Maybe it was the sound of the balls thudding against the walls of the rec room, or the squishing sound they made when they found the foam-soaked carpet, or the sound of breaking glass when one of the billiard balls likely crashed through Bea Arthur's smug, back-lit face on the marquis above the game action of the pinball melee.

Dan could not be sure. He was already halfway to the infirmary, hazmatted agents streaming past him toward the noises.

They were anonymous in their complete protection, anthropoid objects decked out in streams of color borrowed from the red neighborhood of the color spectrum.

They could be robots, Dan mused.

One more stop on the way.

"Doc!" Dan declared, busting into the side office of the infirmary. Doctor Marko, confined to the Mansions via the quarantine, jerked in his cushy office chair. "Give me your ID. I'm going to up to where they're hiding Jake, or what's left of him."

"Mr. Nickle, you need to leave."

Dan stepped forward and lowered an index finger he knew must look something like the digits the Wicked Witch angled at Dorothy when she spat out threats at the pre-pubescent Jayhawk and her mutt. "Jake was one of us, and they have no business with him. And if you have any sense beyond what they whipped into you at med school, you know what I know; these guys ain't no FEMA or CDC, and Ike-the-Kike was one of us, riding this Viking barge to Valhalla, sailing waves of daiquiris and sunsets to the accompaniment of syrupy ukulele strums."

"Dan--"

"Tell them I scared you. Tell them I got a tough background. Tell them I'm with the CIA and I was the guy on the grassy knoll," Dan said, sighting down the length of a Margaret Hamilton finger. "Tell them whatever you like. They ain't FEMA, and I ain't leaving here without that ID."

Marko sighed and produced the card.

He was up the stairs, a little breathless but no problem, and at the upper door. He froze. He could not help envisioning gallons of slithering apostrophes waiting just beyond the doorway to the upper level of the domed infirmary.

Sick of the whole business, Dan grunted and thrust his way upward through the door that belonged capping a storm cellar.

A stack of evac gurneys stood along one wall where Jake's bed had been. There were translucent, plastic Walmart packing drawers with various, yet-to-be-used medical supplies.

No Jake. No worms in a glycerin broth.

"Mr. Nickle."

Dan knew the voice. It was the Major.

"What did you do with him?"

"Mr. Nickle. Dan, will you come with me?"

Dan jerked back the arm the Major tried to rest a hand on, likely to gently guide Dan out of the now empty quarantine zone.

But Dan suddenly felt frail, like his skin would rip beneath the Major's powerful grasp. He wasn't nearly that old. He knew old fogies got that way, skin like paper. He wasn't there, yet. But he felt vulnerable all the same.

"What did you do with him, and don't give me this FEMA shit!"

The Major held out his gloved hands. He smelled faintly of cigars. "Please, Dan," the Major pleaded, his voice contrite gravel. "Keep it down, for the sake of the others. Lord knows you and Sue are cut from a different cloth. I can see that now. Tell you what--"

"You're going to tell me right now! What in Hades is going on around here!"

The Major stepped up close so the cigar smoke floated out his large pores into Dan's eyes, making them water a bit. And, maybe, he had already started to cry.

The Major just got quieter and more placative, flat water on the Gulf. He could be hiding anything. "Tell you what, Dan. I could do it." His voice was like the big trucks on the gravel road when they take their time. "I can see you're not giving me a way out of that. So, if you and Sue will come with me--"

"To what? Disappear?"

The Major chuckled, but sucked back any trace of irony from his rain-on-a-tin roof voice. "I'll give you the whole show, Dan. Now hold on, hold on, I'm going to give you the whole show, lift the veil, so to speak. I will unblock yours and Ms. Mayfield's cell phones. How's that? Take a little walk with me and we will both be satisfied. You'll get the straight dope, and you'll give me your word. Deal?"

If asked later, Dan could not swear to what he said to that, but sure as rain in Florida, moments later, Dan allowed himself to be marched through the long, single floor hallways of the Mansion, picking up Sue along the way, and out the front door.

It wasn't until he felt the burn of the sun, that Dan shook himself a bit and faced his partner in crime. *Where are we going?* She mouthed.

Dan shrugged.

But they did go, and kept going. Two residents walking out the front gate of the (friendly, white picket fence variety) old age home named for a vacation rocker and across the dusty lines of the gravel road to nuzzle up to the tangled, impermeable membrane of chain link surrounding the facility across the road.

From this new vantage he could see a sign--planted on a brick wall at an angle not necessarily intended to be seen from the road--that read BioFlouretics.

What the fuck? It could not be less clear if the sign bore a big, black *X*.

And what did FEMA have to do with this place? It was all bullshit, just as he and Gil had suspected from the beginning.

The Major did not knock. Did not enter a code. He did not give a hand signal. The gate simply rolled open. It was a big gate. It took a while.

Sue bumped shoulders with Dan and hooked a thumb in the direction of the Mansions, where, except for select field trips (spring training games were good: Phils and Jays just around the corner) they spent every moment of their lives, sun-up to sundown. *Let's go*, her silent mouth said. She did get the lipstick right. How come she was the only woman in the Mansions who knew where her lips ended?

"I have to know," Dan said aloud.

Playing the affable host, the Major raised a giant hand and let it land across Dan's shoulders. "Of course you do," he said. Dan could not see inside the suits of the retinue of agents flanking them, but they moved together as if rehearsed. "And, as neighbors, you deserve the truth."

It was Dan's turn to take Sue by the elbow and usher her forward into the first brick building (not many in Florida), where the central AC was pumped up to industrial strength. Sue clutched at Dan, and he was grateful for the mutual warmth. He was a bit surprised he could not see his breath.

Not far from this place was the Tampa Aquarium. Dan knew it because of infrequent visits with the grandkids. It was a good place for kids. This place was like that in that it was low lit, with glass tanks embedded in walls of concrete and corrugated steel. Workers of both genders idled between these tanks. Like in an aquarium, or museum, they entered onto a ramp that only allowed for a uni-directional tour.

It was almost as if they had this all set into motion; Sue and he strolling up a defined walkway toward large tanks of water with mood lighting.

"Doctor Oldbridge!" The Major called out to one of the white coats as if by incidental association. "Could you help us out a moment?"

Dr. Oldbridge was a young woman with long blonde hair in a bouncy ponytail. Her white coat covered all but her feet.

"I was told to show you guys around," she said. Her face below the tight crown of blonde hair was open and smiling. She did not wear glasses. She was short and young. She was not convincing as a scientist.

Dan stood his ground. "You guys are not FEMA." It was not a question.

Oldbridge looked briefly at her shoes; the wide smile never slipping from her essentially pretty face.

"No," she said, "we're not FEMA."

Sue raised her hand unconsciously, straightening her glasses with the other hand. "Then what--?"

Oldbridge made a gesture with her left arm, straight out toward the Minor Mansions escapees, indicating to come along, allow themselves to be enfolded into her diminutive care. Her clipboard was gripped tightly in her right hand. "Come with me," she said. "Let me show you."

Sue eyed Dan who shrugged. They were here, weren't they? And, he wanted to know.

Oldbridge's outstretched arm only floated inches from Dan's back, but it seemed to usher them forward all the same. The tour ramp angled up and around a corner, deep into the facility. All along the wall were tanks filled with water and vegetation typical to the clogged waterways all around shoreline regions, Florida lying low like a supine cow, inviting the surrounding Gulf into her.

But it wasn't until they rounded the corner, out of the natural lighting from long windows in the entryway into what essentially was a warehouse, that the tanks were carefully lit to reveal and highlight the creatures that lived within. The hallway was dark and the tanks, Dan thought, were pretty. It was as though something built for tourists.

The first tank had a single occupant, floating noncommittally through the fronds of kelp, swaying in an artificial wave pattern.

"The New Zealand long-finned eel," the young scientist said.

The tank looked good. The lighting was good. The glass was immaculate as was the water that held the dozing eel. And, it was lie.

Sue's mouth was an open 'O'. "Is that what attacked Jacob? Made him sick?"

"We believe--"

Dan waved off the blond. "Bullshit," he said, "it's all bullshit."

"Mr. Nickle--"

Dan turned to Sue. "Not FEMA," he said, pointing a crooked finger at Oldbridge. "And that is not the thing I saw down in the drainage ditch. And I saw plenty."

Now it was the young scientist's turn to drop her mouth to open gape. "Mr. Nickle, I can assure you--"

"Skip the tour, sweetheart, who are you people and what are you up to out here?"

The small hand Oldbridge held up in protest had short nails, no polish. Dan waved off the gesture. "Listen," he said, "I've seen one of those things, and that ain't it."

Oldbridge nodded, her ponytail bouncing. "Yes, you have."

"Maybe," Dan said, "maybe I haven't been quite as forthcoming with you people about what I know and what I've seen. I'm no scientist, but if experiments are what you people are up to, then I'm sure you'd like a detailed report on exactly what I saw happening to Jake over at the infirmary. So should we call the Major back and cut the bullshit?"

Young Dr. Oldbridge looked the old man up and down, pursing her lips and doing some loose calculations behind her hazel eyes.

"I don't think that will be necessary, Mr. Nickle," she said. "Come this way."

Dan grunted satisfactorily and followed the short woman further into the dark of the tour, to a crash door that allowed them back into the open light of the warehouse, and into a room of many tanks, roiling with bubbles from powerful aerators. There were no decorative plants in these tanks. The glass of each tank looked like it could use a good wipe-down. The creatures in these tanks were small, smaller and smaller as one walked the gamut of austere aquariums. The final tanks seemed infested with living exclamation points, loosened from the pages of a very intense story.

Oldbridge stopped at these tanks and eyed Dan, checking his satisfaction level.

"Not eels?" Dan said.

"No," said Oldbridge.

"And you folks have no connection to the CDC or FEMA?" Sue asked.

Oldbridge shook her head. "No," she said. "We are a private corporation working under government control, top secret, like companies that design and build parts for military hardware."

"And these are definitely not eels," Dan announced triumphantly.

"Well," Dr. Oldbridge said, "the New Zealand long fin does have the capability of crossing some impressive stretches of land in order to maximize the spread of egg clusters into various wet spots over their territory. Long fin exists on several islands of lower Malaysia, including Australia. A spring stroll in Perth is often interrupted by the crawling presence of long, black eel."

Sue bent at the waist to get a closer look. "So these are…"

"The chief contributor to this species is the long fin eel."

Dan turned to the scientist. "Contributor? Then these are some sort of genetically altered freaks?"

Oldbridge shrugged. "For a lack of a better term, yes. Of the lines we have in production, these have been the most successful, performing according to plan."

"What plan?" Dan asked. "Whose plan?"

A deep voice resounded throughout the vast space. "A design created by the company according to specs by our client," the Major said from behind them.

"And who is that?" Dan asked.

The Major raised his arms to their full condor spread. "That's classified, Dan."

"But," Sue began, "don't you think we're owed something of an explanation? These top secret experiments are happening right outside our home and one of them got away."

"No I don't, Ms. Mayfield. No I don't." The Major approached the old woman, looming over her. "We were here before Minor Mansions. If the last president hadn't been such a big fan of daiquiris and Bermuda shorts, the rest of the peninsula would never have, and should never have been deeded away."

"Damn it, man," Dan spat. "We're Americans too!"

"And as Americans, you gotta know; business is business. Everybody gotta do business. Just as Darren Minor. You think he opened that place out there to reward his fans or just bleed them one last time with the ultimate merchandising, daq-head utopia."

Dan did not have an argument for that, but neither was he appeased. "Sounds like we got a problem then," he said. "The Mansions being across from your mad scientist lab seems like an invitation toward tragedy, and our place is on the news a lot. Minor Mansions is one of a kind. Hard to cover up messes like we had with Jake."

The Major seemed to consider. "What do you propose, Dan?"

Dan put his spotted hand to his hips. "Your client is the US government? NSA? CIA?"

"You know I can't tell you that, Dan."

"Let me ask you one question then, Major," Dan said. "These eel things, they have any direct use? Are they gonna be used tomorrow in Afghanistan or somewheres?"

The Major made a smacking sound with his lips. "Nothing we've worked on here has been used, no. What we make here are extreme contingency capabilities, one that would be too strange to be believed. Ironically, this could allow the user to operate more in the light. But it seems as though…"

There was a brief silence. The aerators hummed next to them.

Dan frowned. "They're afraid to use these. They're abominations that no one can control. Could turn a whole, what: village? County? Country?--into what Jake was at the end. What happened to him?"

Dr. Oldbridge spoke almost excitedly. "What we have here is something more akin to a macro-virus than any known species. They can spread themselves exponentially through their bite--" The Major put a huge, dark hand on her shoulder. "That's enough, Doctor," he said. "What are you driving at, Dan?"

"I'm guessing you don't need a whole warehouse of these things," he said. "You probably don't even need live animals. Just freeze a few and make more when called upon."

The Major put his hands behind his back in an exaggerated at-ease position. He looked to the corrugated steel ceiling, then at the scientist. "Doc, a word outside?"

The short woman nodded and followed the Major to stand across from them on the other side of the rows of fish tanks, out of earshot.

Dan dug into his pocket and found a tube of lip balm.

Sue's brow knotted. "Your lips bothering you that badly?"

Dan screwed the protective gel to the top and then ripped it out of the tube. He twisted the bottom of the dispenser to open the tube back up. He stepped over to one of the tanks and reached.

Sue gasped and looked down the long row of tanks where the tall soldier and the short scientist were talking heatedly.

"Dan!" she hissed, grabbing for him.

"I'm taking one of these things."

She tried to keep her voice below a shocked scream. "What? NO!"

Their hosts were still talking down the row.

"We need something, just in case." He was fishing around among a shoal of black, squirming figures swimming through wreaths of aerator bubbles. "Someday these guys are going to get us killed, and I want my family to know why. Gotcha!"

He removed his hand, cupped to hold onto the apparently wiggling thing inside. He raised the empty balm tube, but when he opened his cupped fist, there was nothing there.

"Uh-oh," he said, turning his hand, looking for where he may have accidently squished the little creature. He turned his hand just in time to see the dark, slithering shadow slip beneath the top layer of his specked skin and begin swimming under the epidermis like a child hiding under a blanket. Then it was gone completely, having dived into the deeper tissues of the hand. Dan felt a tickling buzzing in his right hand.

It was inside him.

"Shit," he said.

SIX

Perhaps with Dan's meltdown in mind, the Major seemed rather genial and conciliatory as though he was herding kindergarten children. He gently escorted the two old friends from the facility.

Sue looked at her sneakers the whole time.

"We run tours every Wednesday and Saturday," he said once the two old folks were on the other side of the property line.

"Really?" asked Sue.

"No." The Major turned as the high chain link gate rolled to a close.

Once the tall black man was out of sight, Sue grabbed Dan and hurried him across the road. "Come on!"

"To where?" Dan asked.

"To…" She had no idea. "To Doctor Marko."

Dan held out his right hand, gripping hard around the wrist with his left as though applying a tourniquet with his gnarled fingers.

"I can feel it in there," Dan said.

Sue felt an electric sense of alarm spread through her, as though she too had been invaded by some squirming creature.

"Come on, Daniel!"

But she was not so sure there was anywhere to go.

They scuffed quickly across the gravel, kicking up pellets of dust. Dan moaned loudly. "Ah! Help, me Sue, please!"

She got him onto Minor Mansions property, a sprawling lawn fed by an armory of sprinkler heads, but he'd go no farther.

Sue searched for her voice and for a course of action. Mother to three and grandmother of five, a calm response to the tragic and near tragic came with the territory. That's why she felt shame at her reaction to Dan and the thing that had impregnated him. The single, long hump swimming under the specked skin of Dan's bare forearms became three, then five, then more.

Sue remembered how Dan described what had happened to Jacob, how he had become a nest for these things. Sue put a hand to her mouth to stifle the scream building there and stepped back from Dan.

Her old friend (and had she wanted it to be more?), became a gurgling hive of slithering bulges until his right arm, looking like Popeye after mainlining a melange of spinach and roids.

Sue Mayfield backed away, some part of her deeply ashamed, but she kept back peddling across the kempt lawn of the Mansions. Her eyes locked on the horror before her. Sue tripped over a sprinkler head and went down. Her dentures clacked together, nearly spilling from her mouth as she landed with a thud.

Dan continued to bulge strangely, flesh undulating spasmodically. The whole ballooning of the right arm traveled to the left and back. Dan stopped screaming, could not scream, as somewhere in the passage between hemispheres, the unseen, rapacious infestation ate through his vocal chords. Then it was all an aggressive series of expansions and contractions. Sue told herself to look away but failed. She lifted an arm to protect herself from the badness she knew was coming. This too failed.

Dan exploded.

Sue let go her scream. She screamed up at the flight of clear sluice splashing out of something unrecognizable as a human being, one she had known well. She fired her scream at it to stop it--clearly run through with viral tadpoles--a tsunami of creeping threat. She tried to scream it away, only to become aware that her gaping mouth allowed for uninterrupted ingestion of the wave about to soak her with amniotic fluid of damnation. She could not close her mouth or she too would swell with black screams.

There was a click behind her. The sprinklers came on. The water was cold and the jet stream powerful. Dan's ruined trunk fell as the sprinkler stream beat back the spray of baby eel-things.

Sue stopped screaming, breathing hard, too hard, breathing run-amok. Her chest complained.

Ibis nested in the mangrove surrounding, nearly choking the estate. They chirped their weird song to bring Sue into a moment of strange silence.

Pretty, she thought, not sure what she meant. Any number of things, she supposed. "Florida is pretty," she said, aloud, trying to break back into reality and failing at this too.

The sound of tires on gravel brought her part of the way back.

More BioFlouretic agents come to clean this up, sweep whatever was left of Dan Nickle completely into oblivion; even the worms that ate him won't be left.

Her head lolled hazily in the direction of the front gate, a garden gate, by the front horseshoe drive. These were big vehicles, not the black SUV's that escorted the behemoth dumptrucks. No, these were a caravan of VW buses, and they were coming directly to Minor Mansions.

"Wha…?" she asked the shocked air.

Whoever it was, they moved from a caravan of VW buses and pushed through the frilly garden gate like they owned the place in their mix of ankle-tight skater pants and Hawaiian shirts, old rockers still trying to find the edge.

The tall guy in the lead, unlike his crew, was old and wore his age with unabashed leisure. He wore shorts. His stride was long. Before too long he held out a long hand to Sue to invite her to a standing position.

"Help you to a vertical, darlin'?"

When he had successfully got his charge onto the soles of her arch-support sneakers, he looked around the area.

"What the fuck happened here?" he asked. He inclined his soul patch at the remains of Dan Nickle, a set of legs with white hairs sheathed in cargo shorts. "A little early for Halloween, dude."

Sue tried to focus on the man. "Who…?"

"Hey!" he said, holding out a hand for a handshake. "Maybe you heard of me? I'm Darren Minor. I own this place, like a lot of places I own. But, I heard there was trouble here. So, here I am."

Sue wondered how to turn a scream into articulate communication. "I…I…the…eels…"

Minor glanced around. "Oh, yeah." He did not seem impressed. "What the fuck are those?"

***

One of them had a flamethrower, or something like it, and Sue couldn't help wondering why anyone travelled with a flamethrower. She was grateful though, oh yes, like the dead, grateful.

"The lawn…" was all she got out. Minor, the tall refugee from 1971, misconstrued her meaning.

"Don't worry, babe. Like I said, I own this joint. It's named after me."

"You're Darren Minor."

"We've established that." His many associates poured from the sliding doors of VW vehicles with alternating panels of cream and orange. "Any of them left?"

"Uh-huh, boss," the associate with the flamethrower reported.

Sue blinked. A clearer look at the device showed it wasn't really a flamethrower in the military sense but something like a toy, something a twelve-year-old piro would rig together, all naked cage-match cylinders and livestock barbed wire.

Was Dan real? Was any of this real? Was this really Darren Minor holding my hand?

"I saw you in seventy-four at old Riverfront Stadium. You did two encores."

"Yeah," the vacation-rock god blurted, "those were the times. We blew through curfews pretty regular back then."

Sue pointed at the lawn, had lost a clear sense of where Dan had fallen. "He was my friend."

She stared at the spot and could not move. She did not budge when one member of the Minor road crew tried to save her from the singed lawn. Minor pitched in, taking one of her arms.

"Come on, girl," he said, "this Florida sun will have you done in in three shakes."

"But…"

She did not know how many of them it took, but they moved her.

Residents first took the Minor crew as the return of the supposed government response agency. Then someone bellowed, "It's the Narcs!"

But then the titters sizzled narcoleptically through the throngs of argyle-over tie-dye. It was as though the visit from the hazmatters had been a prelude, a prankster warm-up crew for the main act. And it had been worth the wait, as though they had been waiting to do anything but die.

A chant went up; how easily, how silently the disturbing events of the morning transmuted into unremitting ecstasy.

"The sun goes down! The sun goes down! The sun goes down!"

Sue knew the source of the chant but could not connect the brain dots to care.

Prolonged sunsets, so sweet and rich in the scarlet slice of the spectrum, serving only to enliven the beer glass hosting some last bits of crescent sliced ice cubes and a tangerine sluice of rum and any other substance that may have snuck in via backwash or visiting insect.

The throng of the Mansions saw these things; it was in the eyes shimmering behind eyeglasses the size of beer mugs. They came to their feet, not seeing Sue Mayfield as passenger to their hero's caravan.

Their absentee children forgotten, the cost of years on knees that would no longer even let them play the diminished golf course where a black slimy thing found that thug, Ike-the-kike. Whatever happened to him, no one cared.

"The Sun Goes Down!"

Then three of them did go down, never getting to a full upright position where they, perhaps, imagined themselves knocking about a beach ball and hunting down a bottle of nitrous. There weren't enough orderlies to catch them all.

Darren Minor briefly raised his arms in triumph of reconnecting with his people, truly his now, none likely to leave his Gulf Coast nirvana.

Sue's knees started to give way when the tall yacht rock god remembered his burden.

He ushered her away from the hosts of ancient followers, collapsing like flamingo-colored dominoes.

"Come on, girl."

He knew where the director's office was, heck, he knew where everything was; he'd poured over spec blueprints for months before approving the final plan. Never spent a night here, though.

He lowered the old woman into a half-back chair and hobbled a bit over to the director's swivel chair.

Sue wondered absently if Diane, the head-honcho of this place, hadn't taken an extended vacation the second Jake had been found on the pathetic golf course.

Someone handed her a glass of water. "Here, chicky."

Chicky?

Had she traveled back to the days of embroidered, beaded vests and buckskin boots and little else. Is that what Darren Minor had created here, on this somewhat out-of-the-way spot on the Gulf Coast? A doorway to the years the 1960's forgot to take with them when they fled into history? Here, the Band was still touring, John and Yoko invited war to stay in bed with them and never leave. This was the time when Darren Minor had made his bones and had become one of the most sought after touring acts of the late Vietnam era.

You could go back to that time, Sue thought, *you just had to let a few eel demons eat some of the passengers. Small price.*

Minor bent, his knees crackling like gravel beneath VW bus tires. He stroked her hand as she sipped at the water and invited her to take big, relaxing breaths.

"Sue, baby, Sue?"

She took long breaths, too long, intakes of atmosphere with no terminus. She kept gulping air and looking to a far away place beyond the pastel ceiling. "I saw you the first time at Pimlico. A girlfriend of mine was going to college near there. I didn't like jam rock or smoothed out stuff, but, man, you guys could play."

She did not look him in the face. Even when the aging rocker took her by the chin and forced her to look him in the famous baby-blues, she was still looking at some far away place, seeing him as he was then, long haired and tanner than a plank of well-oiled cherry wood.

He snapped thick fingers in front of her unseeing eyes. Nothing.

Sue felt something electric across her face.

"Sure hated to do that, babe."

Her face stung. He had slapped her.

"Sorry, babe, but you--"

"They're out there," she said, not all the way back, yet. "They're out there, so many."

"Whatever they were, Gabe got 'em. He used to do pyrotechnic work for Black Sabbath."

"No." Sue said, standing and going to the window. She thrust aside the velour blinds. "No! There!" She pointed at the industrial plant across the road. "They're out there."

The office door knocked open with a violent clunk. Gabe was there, he of the homemade flamethrower and dirty bandana. He had another member of the Minor posse with him. Sue gasped deeply at the way the second man was holding his arm.

It could be he broke his arm, that's all, she told herself. But she knew better. They're out there.

Gabe had a solid grip high on the other's arm as though trying to stop a leak in a balloon.

Both men looked scared. "We got a problem, boss."

Sue stared, mute; she tried to scream out the all-consuming terror welling up in her, but her mouth would only allow a shuddering ululation that grew in intensity.

The great king of songs about sunsets split his attention between the clearly insane woman and his injured pal. Sue forced herself to move when the first wiggling, black form pushed its way out of the man's skin.

"Holy Jesus!" Gabe, the flamethrower man, cried.

Sue pushed past them, now letting a genuine scream precede her into the gently carpeted, tight hallways.

She had to get out of this place.

Who sang that song?

Were cellphones working yet? She didn't take any chances. The rest of the residents were all atwitter, some requiring medical attention from the nurses in order to manage their glee.

This meant the nurse's station was clear and so was the phone mounted to the wall just around the wall hosting the pill schedule. Sue did not bother walking around into the work space but, instead, leaped like a Seaworld seal onto the counter and ripped the receiver from the cradle. Phones in the Mansions still had twist chords. She made some unhinged attempt to dial, and when failing to get her various limbs to work independently of her shattered mind, started yelling into the receiver.

She called her oldest daughter's name, like a lost child, helplessly bellowing for its parent in a giant world that had suddenly turned sinister.

"Angela! You have to come get me! Angela! The eel wranglers, they're back! This awful, awful place. They grow them. I don't know why. Why would anyone make such things? Is the world not horrible enough? Angela?"

Many figures were running then. If she kept on yelling into the phone, by some strange law of improbability, she'd reach her daughter. No one cared about her here. As soft as the music was and as bright as the colors were, Dan had been her only friend--her nursing home husband. Now he had been eaten by monster worms that were only getting started.

"Angela!"

She screamed and screamed, at some point hoping someone, anyone, a nurse, would stop her, drag her off to her room and dope her so deeply she wouldn't feel the worms running through her like old meat left out in the sun.

But no one stopped her, and as she screamed herself somewhat lucid, when it became clear she could not really pull herself together to work the old phone and that her daughter wasn't going to come and save her (she'd only seen Angela's family once in the three years), she looked about to witness a sort of chaos to rival her temporary madness.

The Major's platoon of hazmats had returned, and they seemed to be in mortal combat with the sandaled Darren Minor entourage.

SEVEN

Here was another of the fantastic devices the BioFlouretics agents had available to them--a buzz stick so powerfully electrified, it could cut through living tissue including bone. No problem. Zip!

Apparently this is exactly what happened to the afflicted member of the Minor militia.

A reciprocal reaction erupted from the other members of the Darren Minor road crew when they witnessed the removal of the lower end of the man's arm (and the subsequent screaming from the man, now unconscious) as an assault. Careless of who may have harmed one of their own, the Minor crew produced their own cache of weapons. Chains swung out and ripped at hazmat fabric but did even more damage to the artwork on the walls around the lobby. Glass flew from collages of fake oil prints, featuring Minor on various feel good tours. Black, steel batons flipped out and knocked agents to the ground as well as breaking vases full of fake flowers. BioFlouretic agents cut the air with their bush beating sticks, causing equal damage and sending the residents into gape-mouthed panic.

Gil Enchevia grabbed his chest and dropped to the ground. When Nurse Struman rushed to his side, she took some kind of projectile in the back and lay atop her patient.

Sue, drawn out of her own shock, knew there was another threat here, one that could be growing while these two groups of men took out their secret need for violence on each other.

She stepped away from the nurse's station, holding her hands in protest. A large figure stepped in front of her. "Hold your fire!" the Major bellowed into the melee. The battle went on. He was joined by the relaxation rocker himself--just as tall as the Major, but a bit hunched with age and all wire.

"Dudes! Chill!"

Still no reaction. Something tiny whizzed by Sue's grey head and took a six inch hole out of the drywall behind her without making a sound. The hole smoked.

The Major produced something from one of the many Velcro-secured pockets on his paramilitary uniform.

He whispered something to Minor, who nodded and stuck his fingers in his hairy ears. When the large black man triggered the button on top of what looked like a birthday candle, a seismic bolt went through Sue's head.

For the hazmat agents, it was a familiar signal, a conditioned response. Regardless of what their opponents may have had up their sleeve at that moment, the discipline of the men from Flouretics drew them to attention, totally vulnerable to the blows of the Minor posse. Except, they were all on their knees, or leaning heavily against the nearest door jam; all of them holding their ears. The senior citizens were out, dead out.

Sue swayed but managed to keep her feet under her.

"Gentlemen," the Major announced, removing an earplug from each ear. "Our good Ms. Mayfield, is correct. We are on the clock here against an enemy with no known containment."

Minor had taken the time to stick in his ear buds he usually plugged into the board, replacing stage monitors. "Hey, guys! Our soldier friend here is right; we're into pretty weird shit, clearly. But this is the crew that negotiated bobcat pass, three days gone on shrooms and Twizzlers. No one is steeped deeper in weird than we are."

"Hey, Mine-man," one of the posse said.

Mine-man? Sue thought. *Someone needs to remind me why I ever listened to this guy.*

That member of the posse, did Sue know his name? Should she? He persisted with the point he seemed to struggle to lock onto. "Hey, Dare, dude, this might be out there, even for us. Did you get a look at what's erupting out there, like a guy exploding into black worms. Like, I had a puppy with worms. I'm not saying it's like that; I'm saying this is like nothing you've ever seen, man."

Minor chuckled. "Wasn't I the guy that took that chick, you remember her? The chick with the third nipple and tried to sell her like a bovine hybrid back in the days of desert gigs by roadside stands, those proto-burning man gigs? You know, I'm the leisure king, the king of the all-inclusive resort and the marimba house band set list. Need I remind you?"

"What…" Sue started, but had to regain her feet. The Major's sonic stunner and its effects were still a distant, numbing effect. "We need to…"

Minor thrust a hand in the air, as if a stage dive was imminent. "Absolutely!"

Absolutely.

Sue stepped into the mix. Just behind her the still figure of Gil Enchevia lay on the floor, a smashed bug under the now vertical nurse. "It's them!" Sue declared, an accusing finger leveled at the much taller figures in the general vicinity of the lobby. "These things were made by them!" The accusation was leveled at the Major.

He remained a wrought iron in fatigues. "There is only one thing we have available to us men."

"The Chicxulub Protocol, sir?"

To Sue the voices came from several directions, all of them unintelligible. This last one, sounded slightly muffled by a hazmat filter.

For the first time, the Major breathed and flustered, produced one of his cigars and used it as a pointer, or safe word. "Chixc. I'm afraid so, my darlings. That's where we are."

Minor watched, Sue observing. Finally the tall, thin man extracted his spidery fingers from the pockets of his Bermuda shorts. "You heard the man!"

One of his posse seemed almost to protest. "Chicxulub, I mean…"

The Major interrupted. "Follow us!"

Neither of the testosterone fed groups seemed at all concerned with the slowly recovering seniors, just now settling themselves into plush furniture peeking out from a healthy growth of bamboo housed in narrow box gardens.

Sue felt mild surprise at how willingly the Minor crowd fell in behind the mysterious and (as Sue identified them) nefariously hazmatted agents of BioFlouretics. "Wait until you see," she called after them.

The Major and Minor looked at Sue and then exchanged knowing glances. "Ms. Mayfield--"

Sue angled a tense finger at their backs. "You better not get in your heads that you're leaving me behind. Dan was my friend, and this is, whether I like it or not, where I live. It's our home! And what concerns our home, concerns me. And, may I point out, it's a little late to cut me out of the loop so kill me now and tell my family I died in my sleep, whatever, *but I am coming!*"

The two giants tossed another bit of ESP between them and smiled like a couple of smart-alecks. "I was about to say," the Major said, grinning, "we couldn't imagine continuing without your assistance."

Sue lifted her chin high. "Damn straight."

***

The Minor road crew was taken through the same tour of tanks and eels, some the genuine article, big black coiling things the length of one of Darren Minor's grasshopper legs and slick as the truth on the floor of Congress. Doctor short and perky was waiting for them at the long room of aggressively aerated tanks and swirling devil worms, definitely not eels.

The hazmats disappeared into various narrow gaps in the room that apparently led to back rooms and secret spaces between walls. While visible, their all-covering suits remained.

One of the Minor crew tapped on the glass of one of the roiling worm tanks. Sue went rigid.

"Don't!" The sound echoed around the warehouse. Her heart was beating like a machine gun. But the fool stepped away, and that was the important part.

She must have been breathing hard, because the Mine-man himself came over and put a spindly arm around her shoulder. "Easy, darlin'."

"Those are what got Dan," she said, massaging the harried pulse at her neck.

Minor peered into the swirling bubbles. "Those? Hmm, they do look sorta like what was in the front yard of my place. Those are eels?"

"No," Sue said, pointing. "Those are monsters. They make monsters here."

A deep, resonant voice spoke from behind. "Actually, we found those." The Major sidled up and then looked to bouncy little Sarah Oldbridge, handing off the rest of the story to the young scientist.

"It's what we found, after we went in to recover our missing team, about four hundred nautical miles past point-bravo, the no-man's land for oil rigs."

"Team of what?" Minor asked.

The Major and Oldbridge simultaneously lifted their eyebrows. "Research," they said in unison, looking rather silly to Sue but not all that ashamed of their naked falsehood.

Minor nodded. "Uh-huh, that's what we used to call it when we'd down a tab of the brown before that show at Red Rocks, flipping out on the power of that clear, Colorado sky. It was research into how fantastic life can be."

No one seemed to have a response to this. But Sue sensed that there was a story the BioFlouretics emissaries wanted to deliver, "What kind of research?"

"New ways to soak oil out of the big cradle called the Gulf of Mexico, no doubt," the do-ragged member of the Minor crew, the one who'd tapped on the glass of the killer worms, said.

Oldbridge said nothing.

Minor took off his tinted glasses, gave them a wipe on his Hawaiian shirt and popped them back on his long nose. "Don't think so," he said. "I think we are being given an invitation."

Sue got a big gulp of air conditioned atmosphere. "Invitation to do what?"

"Not to go deeper on this, Ms. Mayfield," the Major said. "We have an admission to make and there are elements of this that are swirling out of our hands, and, because some numbnuts made that land available across the road to one of the most recognizable figures in America today, we here at the company have been, rather rapidly, backed into a corner."

"You can't clean this up quietly anymore, can you?" Minor said. "I made that impossible."

The Major nodded. "Indeed."

"I'm sure you have a number of methods available to you to discourage our involvement," Minor said.

The Major cleared his throat. "We do. And I'm going to invoke one of those methods now."

"I can't disappear!" Sue cried. "People will know!"

"You don't get it," the Major said.

Oldbridge piped in, "We don't have time to focus on two fronts. We need containment, not just of the entities. There is no time to deal with the chaos of mass hysteria. We need containment on information too. Ms. Mayfield, you are the real problem."

Sue cringed. "You can't--"

The Major held up a hand to stop Sue's worst fears from taking complete hold of her. "It's a compliment, really," he said. "Unlike all your pals at the residence, you have a lot on the ball."

Minor shook his gray locks in Sue's direction. "She's too wily to let go, and I'm too famous."

Dr. Oldbridge nodded. "This is scary, but we can't have you guys back out. We need you to dive in all the way. We can't guarantee you'll ever understand what is happening, either way."

"Because you don't?" Minor asked.

The Major ignored this. "And, we can't guarantee your safety, whatever you choose. This is a hot zone now. And your elder care facility there is part-and-parcel with this leg of the battle."

Sue could not stand it any longer. "BATTLE WITH WHAT?"

She did not flinch when her voice bounced back down on her from the metal roof.

"No time for stories, babe," Minor said. "That's what they're trying to tell us. Either go for the full ride or spend the rest of the journey locked in a back room while we wait for the end of the world."

The silence that rolled in chilled the crisp, overly conditioned air of the cavernous building.

"Well," Minor said, glancing around at his guys, "speaking for my crew, we're in. I mean it sounds like you're saying there's no wading in on this, we were hip deep the second we got out of our Volkswagens."

The Major nodded. "Once the entities were confirmed in the drain pipe feeding out into the bay, certain protocols became functionally automatic."

Sue gripped her arms protectively to her chest. "But I don't have to come...wherever? To do...whatever?"

"All your friends across the road don't know a thing," Oldbridge said. "You can't rejoin them until it's over; it would do untold harm. Or, you can come along and help us out."

Sue rubbed frantically at her hair and throat, then wrung her hands until they were bright red. What would her family think?

***

The thing in the huge fish tank in the middle of the room was a true oddity, but Sue found herself more surprised by the fact that one of the hazmatted agents turned out to be a woman. The various levels of the vacuous facility had more hidden chambers than the Tower of London. A locker room of some sort must be somewhere in the folds. The BioFlouretics agents stood around, monitoring various laptops and eyeing the big tank just as Sue and Darren Minor stood shoulder-to-shoulder, peering through glass so thick it slightly refracted the light penetrating from the other side. The agents now wore fatigue pants with cargo pockets and featureless, black Tshirts. Sue noted the woman agent's shirt had a looser neckline, denoting a woman's cut.

Dr. Oldbridge joined them at the tank. The giant container sprouted from the center of the cement floor, the heavily lidded top looming over them from what Sue guessed to be twenty-feet from the top of Darren Minor's head.

The water swirled to the current created by the monsters sailing about its depths.

Darren Minor swung his long, strumming finger at the big tank. "So, these things, they are, what?"

Oldbridge cleared her throat. "We don't actually know."

Sue shook her head. "You don't know?"

"No," Oldbridge said, "they were discovered about eight years ago out in the Gulf. Do you know what the Gulf of Mexico is, really?"

Sue and the rock god shook their heads. Oldbridge walked up to within a few inches of the thick glass containing the monsters, eight-foot-long black swirls. Sue's breath caught in her throat. "The Gulf of Mexico is an impact crater. It's where a massive meteor struck the Earth's surface, kicking up great amounts of terrestrial materials into all levels of the ancient atmosphere. In a few years after impact, the sudden opaqueness to the stratosphere caused a global temperature drop of six degrees. This meant extinction of many species, most of them plants. The effect got worse as the years stretched on, ultimately causing the mass extinction of thousands of species, most notably a family of creatures known as the dinosaurs."

"So, what's this?" Minor asked. "A dino eel?"

Oldbridge nodded. "These large ones here are what they turn into after devouring each other." Oldbridge turned to face her audience. "It is my theory that this is a species that can exist in conditions known life forms cannot survive in, or at least their genes can, such that they, perhaps, were trapped by the meteor impact, rather than destroyed by it. This species has many strange qualities. You see that this tank has no aeration?"

Sue nodded. "Yeah," she said, "it's awfully quiet in there."

"They don't need it," Oldbridge said. "They don't breathe in any conventional sense. The bubble units in the other tanks is for show, to confuse the curious."

"What else do you know about them?" Minor asked.

Oldbridge signaled to the closest of the corporate agents. "It's easier to show you."

An agent the size of a mountain, followed closely by the much shorter female agent, crossed to a bank of sturdy laptops. Sue had learned her name was Janine. Though a head shorter than her fellow agent, Janine looked to Sue as though she could chew nails and spit out screws.

"There," Oldbridge said, pointing to spouts at the top of the austere container for the animate giants, musical clefs written in a satanic font. A dark spigot extended into the water that looked very cold to Sue. From the spigots a dark fluid ribboned into the swirling water. "That should produce the desired effect."

The fluid slipped down around the monstrosities. Sue could now identify as something closer to leeches. As the substance attenuated, it exposed an aspect of the liquid not at first clear to Sue. The fluid was the color of…

"Blood," Sue said, her jangled nerves chiming like bells.

Dr. Oldbridge seemed calm about it. "Yes," she said, "the key stimulus."

Minor had been rather quiet, rubbing compulsively at the tip of his long nose. "What kind of blood?"

Oldbridge shrugged. "Any will do," she said. "This is porcine, pig blood."

I know what porcine means, Sue thought.

The blood settled on the rolling black masses. Sue reached over and grabbed Minor by the upper arm, perhaps a little too hard, but she couldn't help it. The monsters froze. The water stopped swishing. The room became very still. Minor did not make a noise as Sue dug in with her fingers, sensible cut on the nails.

Like a big clot of hair, Sue thought, examining the now still creatures. m*Gathered on the shower drain of a family with really dark hair.*

The giant pubic strands froze, bolt still then began to shiver, until the crimson tinted water shimmered at the surface of the captive ocean.

The shiver became a shudder, breaking into total seizure, a low hum vibrating through the tank to the concrete floor.

Another squirt of crimson entered the tank.

Oldbridge held an iron rod hand out toward the pair manning the laptops. "Hey!" she grunted. "We already had the maximum in the tank."

The ground shook.

The Major emerged through a door that adjoined a long mirror, that was clearly two sided glass. He stood at the top of a short series of steps, crossed his uniformed arms over his hogshead of a chest.

The agents eyed him nervously.

Pop! Not something audible but felt, the two monsters became three.

Oldbridge had not yet lowered her warning arm. The shivering running through the building seemed to ease and so did Oldbridge, but then the extra squirt of pig blood settled on the recently multiplied super eels.

One of Sue's daughters lived in the foothills of Sacramento, the back alley of wine country, and she reported (rather unconcerned) a regular series of tremors that rumbled the dishes and tumbled brick-a-brac from shelves. Sue always felt nervous at the reports from her middle child.

That was nothing compared to how she felt when the concrete floor, like the floor of a carny haunted house, flicked her away from it, shooting her inches into the air, like a bovine (that means cow) shaking off biting flies.

Now there were four monsters in the tank suddenly looked crowded. The quake erupting in the tank continued unabated.

Sue heard someone call her name. She turned and saw the Major calling her to the stairs leading up to what appeared to be the command center. Sue had hardly taken a step when the first stream of water gouted from a busted seam in the steel frame hosting and supporting the thick glass.

The Major's deep voice became nearly inaudible below the scream of the buttressing frame struts. "Run!"

A hand grasped Sue under the arm and hurried her along. Darren Minor had her and he looked scared.

Something shot past Sue's face. The wash of water over her head told her the tank had blown. She spared a glance at the contents of the tank. Five of the monsters ballooned to every inch of the container.

Sue thought her heart would burst in a similar fashion.

A steel bolt, blown from the pressure of the screaming support frame, ricocheted off the cement floor directly in front of Sue, launching a chip of cement up at her. There was a sting, and then wet warmth. She put a hand to her face and felt the damp of blood.

Better not let those things get a taste, she thought insanely, *or there will be a hundred of them in here.*

Sue held her face as she got a foot on the first metal step, getting off the factory floor just in time to escape the rush of water.

Agents rushed past her, going the wrong direction as far as Sue was concerned. They drew slender sidearms as they closed in on the broken nest of devil eels.

Sue stopped at the top of the steps to see. Without their hazmat Halloween costumes, the agents of this place with the intimidatingly corporate name struck Sue as something personal to her, people she knew in a way that made her forget other people.

She had trouble remembering a time before the moment she watched Dan Nickle explode.

She was old enough to know better. There were things that could not be unseen, but these were people running forward to face monsters with stick guns. One of them was named Janine.

And she was the first to get it. A goliath, hardened proboscis the shade of shark's eyes stretched from the springing heart of an Olympian leech and pierced the smaller agent through the center of her lady's black tee. Death was quiet beneath the hiss of water gushing across the floor.

Major took her other arm, and Sue was removed from the room.

Inside the dark confines of the command center there were a hundred ways to see what Sue really didn't want to see. The noises were many, but there was no way to escape the screaming. Video monitors with surround sound capability were anchored in every corner.

The strange sidearms spat in high whines at the monstrous leeches rolling loose across the floor, stabbing and slamming at the agents as they went.

"There!" Darren Minor said, pointing at a spot on a closed-circuit monitor.

Sue could see the ribbons of blood in the flood.

How many of them would there be when that blood hit them?

Only a single agent served the Major in this, his inner sanctum. He signaled to the well-muscled man now. "Prepare the Clean Sweep protocol."

The agent eyed the Major doubtfully. It sounded ominous and final to Sue, not something that took into account the lives of the agents battling the hell worms.

An eel flopped like a seal across the damp floor, shaped itself into a huge bore bit, and drilled an agent where his two legs met, separating the man at the crotch into several pieces, all of them seemed to be screaming.

Sue turned away. Clean Sweep. Just do it. Please.

There was a button, a red button. The agent's hand hovered. Outside, a black muscle tee tattered into Rorschach shreds. But only the blood mattered. How much blood before these things burst the bounds of the facility?

The well-trained hand waited for the order while living slivers of trepanning bore corkscrewed men into an Escher tangle of black tee meat.

Whatever it is... thought Sue. *For mercy's sake.*

The agent punched the red button.

Hard to say what Sue expected; an intrusive hum? There wasn't even a tell tale glow. The one agent who hadn't been completely eviscerated--merely mortally pierced--crumpled instantly into the two-inch tide of bloody water. The monsters stopped their attack and recommenced a shuddering motion. The shudder evolved into a shiver, violent convulsions and then burst with a traumatic plop that could be heard through the thick walls of the command center.

How badly Sue wished for resolution to a battle she sensed should not have happened, almost as if theater all for her sake-- object lesson in danger. The self that had emerged, the one that rose to talk the grandmother of five out her own consciousness because none of the tough men around her succeeded in helping her hold it together, this self told her to be ready for the next part. This will never be over.

And sure enough, even in the poor resolution of the monitors, the new threat was clear. The wading pool of water in the eel room frothed from the frantic movement of masses of much smaller worms, like the ones that had burst from Jacob and Dan. Small, but so numerous they were easy to discern on the monitors. The shallow skim of water outside now writhed with intricate and innumerable layers of the black things--mini versions of the beasts the red button had destroyed. These little ones were very much alive. The wide tank room had become a cauldron of slimy little leeches.

Sue felt drained and tired. She dabbed at the cut on her face. She thought about asking for a bandage, but something nagged at the back of her mind.

She went to the two-way glass and looked out over the huge puddle covering the floor of the big room; a captive ocean alive with hungry little monsters.

Then it clicked.

Where was the little blonde scientist? There was no lab coat among the tattered clothes floating through the waves of killer worms.

The Major touched the agent at the control panel on a meaty shoulder. "Baker!" It was the agent's name. "Get ready to hit 'em again."

Baker nodded. Sue raised a hand to toss in the question about the scientist. Where was Oldbridge? But just as Sue was turning to face the Major with her concern, a crack formed on the far wall of the tank room. It was a dark, even line.

A door, thought Sue. A door is opening.

Sue spun. "Wait!"

The Major glanced up, his hand instantly tightened on the agent's shoulder.

"Baker, no!"

It was too late. Whatever death ray they had used to break the monster eels into the killer worms had been activated. A short hum and then a click. Oldbridge's short form now clearly visible in the doorway of the hidden hatch across the tank room. The scientist had had the

presence of mind to find the safety of the nearly invisible room, but not the sense to tell anyone.

She fell forward into the water, covered by a skim of black oil, what the worms broke into when given the clean sweep.

EIGHT

Sue sat on a metal container looking out over the busy dock wondering how it was a person got through the looking glass so quickly.

The Minor crew had largely followed Oldbridge into what the Major called the safe room--most days bonus storage for the lab's assundries. Yesterday, for now it was past midnight, the safe room had been used for its name sake, except for Oldbridge's poor timing (she had heard the hum and click of the initial activation of the Clean Sweep device but failed to account for the necessity of the worm mop up), those that had made it behind the thick hatch came out relatively unaffected. There was one road crew member who had a penchant for Panama hats. He still wore it though the left side of the brim, and left ear, looked like it had been melted along with a rather strange tan featured on the same side of his face.

Other than that...

It's a poor sort of memory that only works backwards...

Having a brain is a funny thing, she thought. Having a memory is funnier still. Lewis Carroll knew that and so did her backwards memory.

A little girl bouncing on her knee. "How we doing little Margie?"

Except that had been wrong, she remembered now. It had been Margaret's oldest, Kirsten, Sue had been bouncing on her bony knee. But could she be so certain she hadn't bounced little Margie in just that way when Sue's leg had a little more curve to it? She could not be certain.

It's a poor sort of memory...

She wished for poorer now. How proud she had been--she and Dan both--when they had looked out among the harvest of daq-heads and reckoned their relatively tight screws compared to all the terribly loose ones scattered about the Mansions.

But now she envied the ones who forgot even their own names or what continence felt like.

Dan was the one she could not forget.

The crew worked steadily. Most were not much younger than she, but they were clearly used to a working life and were happy to do some heavy lifting rather than being left to think and remember. They moved as though there was a plan, and Sue understood there was a plan.

The strange vessel now being loaded lay at the center of the intent of that plan, under the aluminum roof of a lengthy boat launch at the back of the plant.

The agents of BioFlouretics, what are they?

The Major could not say, but he knew the next step, their destination--and weren't they all along for the ride? Weren't they all a group born in blood and slimy horror?

Like all the other wonders of BioFlouretics, whatever that was, the vessel was some strange conglomeration of narrow tubes and sleek power. A narrow wonder of metallurgy, the thing floating nearby on the calm waters of the covered boat dock, like all things Flouretic, hid some vast capacity beneath the surface.

And, strangely enough, she was needed on this trip. They were running out of bodies, of witnesses to the properties of the murderous invaders from beyond the Jurassic Era or Hell.

"Sue," the Major's big voice called her back to this world, some looking-glass version of reality. "Ms. Mayfield, grab a couple of these duffles and head aboard."

She was needed. How often had she wished exactly for that from her family, from anyone.

Hadn't that been how she got to this side of the mirror? Jacob Eichkoff had needed her. She knew now; what she needed was to mind her own fucking business.

"Excuse my French." No one heard her. She hoisted the nearest black duffle, stuffed full with something, something heavy.

It was almost comical that she, in her soiled Florida-white sweat pants and coral top, carried heavy bags onto the narrow passageways into the heart of the streamline vessel that she could not tell whether it was a surface ship or a submersible. She was no help at all as it was all hands on deck, men from the Minor crew or Flouretic agents, having to support her all the way. An agent held her elbow as she stepped up onto the narrow deck. A member of the road crew gave her a tight smile as he grabbed her forcibly by the waist and lowered her down into other helpful hands below deck.

The control room was below, telling Sue this marvelous machine would be spending much of its time underwater. Agents had to shimmy to make their way round the tight confines of the many mechanisms with variable hued lights in the dim hold.

All along, accompanying the helpful hands were gentle admonitions offering Sue safe passage through the turmoil of the bridge in the stages of preparation.

Finally, she was ushered into a tight little space that had a set of what looked like recently cleared shelves, the longest of which jutted from the hull at knee level. Sue rested the heavier of the two duffle bags on this feature that pretty much had to be a bunk.

Sue turned to the last of the agents who had carried her this far, still lingering in the doorway. "My suite?"

He tilted his black baseball cap in her direction. "Yes, ma'am," he said.

"I get my own, huh?" she asked, grabbing the zipper of one of the duffles. "This being the bitch berth?"

The agent kicked self consciously at a bit of dirt that was not there. "Hah," he managed, "you know your military, huh? But, uh, no, this is what the specs would have referred to as the captain's quarters."

"Really? The captain's?"

"Yeah, well," he said, hiding beneath the bill of the baseball cap, "this being the only private quarters. Take care ma'am."

He was gone. Sue unzipped the first duffle. There was bedding, ruffled for old ladies.

Sue could not remember if she got sea sick or not.

They were barely out into the Gulf when she was asked to the briefing. She felt some bit of satisfaction that she would not be excluded from inner circle, treated like she was an elderly barnacle.

The men in the room all seemed a bit too tall for the tight quarters, having to find nooks and crannies for their big heads or lean stiffly to fit.

The Major was a giant pole in the center. "We are now a mix-source team, out of last-ditch necessity. The only good part of what has happened is that those involved, civilian and otherwise, have a decent assessment of the stakes."

"Do we?' Sue asked. "As for me, I have no clue what the fuck is going on."

Excuse my French. She was proud she did not voice the apology.

The Major ducked his head from under a pipe. "Fair enough," he said. "As I said, events here on the ground make things pretty clear, to me. And, we all have to be on the same page."

Darren Minor had managed to find a place to sit among the forest of men. "The Major and I had a word," he said to Sue. "We agree it's time for the Major to bring us into the loop."

"Well," Sue said. She allowed her voice all the vinegar she could muster. "As long as you two agree."

The Major sighed. "As you may have guessed." He took the unlit cigar he had between two thick fingers and slid it into a chest pocket. "There is no BioFlouretics."

"Some kind of cover?" Sue asked.

"Hardly," the Major said. "Not a piece of paper indicating its existence. There was never a thought that anyone would enter the facility. Even when you guys moved in next door. The higher ups were reassured when it was discovered…"

"That it was a bunch of old people," Sue said.

The Major held silent for a moment before responding. "This whole operation was put together on the fly by a group run by scientists. In fact, the late Dr. Oldbridge was my boss. A bunch of scholars and researchers, not too big on security. The thinnest cover was established when a few of the specimens almost got away."

"Specimens of what?" Minor asked.

The Major shrugged. "Heck if I know," he said. "I was hired to bring together a private security team. I had some of my own guys I've worked with before and some of those guys put out feelers. That was two months ago. Shortly before that, as is my understanding, the plant was manned with a few workers supporting Dr. Oldbridge. I think, not that I'm in the loop on all this, that is when they discovered the species we all now have encountered."

"They grew them?" one of the music crew asked. "Some kind of mutant, Franken-eels?"

The Major shook his head. "I don't think so," he said. "I'm former black-ops, like a lot of my guys. We were brought in at a pretty penny when it was discovered that containment was an issue. I can tell you, Oldbridge was afraid of these things. And she had every reason to be. As far as I could tell, short of the microwave blaster, something that had been installed before I got there, Oldbridge hadn't made much progress on developing softer options for species control."

"That was her job?" Minor asked. "Develop some kind of eel spray to wipe them out?"

Sue pointed at the Major. The index finger she leveled at him was missing its well-filed nail. "Those things did not come from the plant? Then where do they come from?"

The Major signaled an agent with a point of his broad chin. A map appeared on a narrow flat screen above their heads. It showed a broad satellite enhanced map of the Gulf of Mexico. A small blue dot moved away from the general Tampa Bay region of Florida's west coast. The blue dot made a microscopic move toward a larger red dot near the center of the nearly circular watery region.

"There," the Major said, "that's where they come from and the headquarters for the operation to stop them. It's the epicenter of the incursion. Where they were discovered, and, where there are, from what I've been able to gather, thousands of them out there, waiting."

"Waiting?" Sue asked. "Waiting for what?"

The Major shrugged. "Their chance, I suppose. But that's where we are heading. When Oldbridge went down, the plant was leaderless and no longer of importance. I was ordered to pack up a bunch of materials where Oldbridge had recorded whatever results she had been able to achieve while experimenting on the population she had been given. We're falling back to the operations stronghold, headquarters of a strategy we old soldiers have dubbed Operation Cork."

Minor chuckled. "Does that mean there will be wine when we get there?"

"No," the Major said. "It means if we don't help the scientists keep their overly-educated fingers in the dike, there won't be an ark big enough to save the Earth from this flood."

Sue stayed in her quarters during dinner. No one argued, they simply brought her a tray of warmed tater tots. Having been frozen not long ago, they were mushy.

About the time she managed to get roughly three tots worth of spud down, someone knocked outside her door, a soft accordion slider in a ceiling track. She grunted a welcome around potato sludge, and Darren Minor entered, two bottles of beer wedged between fingers long enough to form a C chord on an elephant's trunk.

He pointed a bottle her way. She nodded, holding out her hand, clear daq-head language for 'where's the bottle opener.' Minor knew the gesture. "It's a screw top."

There wasn't really a place to sit, Minor leaned up against a crate. "You never went on the road, deep daq-head?"

Sue shook her head as she sipped at the beer. It was crap, even to a pedestrian beer drinker like her, but it felt like ambrosia floating down her throat. She suddenly felt very tired. "Saw you guys maybe half dozen times, too middle class to chuck it all and groupie-up."

"They weren't all sluts and space cadets, you know," he said. "But those were good times with folks you didn't mind having a good time with."

Sue sucked a greasy finger clean. "Kinda like now."

Minor laughed so hard, one of his crew, a dude sporting a straw hat, stuck in his face to check on the boss. Minor's laugh, so unabashed and warm caused Sue to chuckle. "Too true," he said, "but you know, you're not far off. You won't see my guys crumbling beneath the weirdest of the weird, ya know?"

Sue nodded, but did not acknowledge beyond the wordless tilt of her now exhausted head.

Minor seemed pressed to get to his point. "I've learned another tidbit from the other crew, the biotech, whatever, guys." He swiped a hand through hair that was still long and lank at the brow, but no longer down to his waist as it was on the *Seven Levels of Chill* tour (generous helpings of gray in the floppy locks too). "They assured me your friend, uh, Stan--"

"Dan."

Minor curtsied submissively. "Hah, yeah, Dan," he said, "good name. Had a guitar tech named Dan. He died of a stroke back in 2001." He shot a look her way, confirmed that the guitar tech mini narrative failed to console and stammered on to his intent. "And! Dan had a real penchant for shrooms. There's a blessing in there, you know. He popped a bass string while tuning a Rickenbacker up for a show in Palo Alto and the fucker went right through the center of his hand, rock-and-roll stigmata, no lie!"

Some part of Sue was sure this was a great story, but right now, she could not catch the tail of this snake. She had no idea why she was hearing this story.

Minor pressed on. "But, but, did that dude worry about it?" He swallowed dramatically at his beer. "Heck no! He sailed so far on his high, he saw roses growing out of his hands. That fucker could slap Spanish tuning on a Walmart guitar in two shakes of groupie tail, but he sure did love his shrooms."

He slapped his thin knee in celebration of the story.

Sue used the sleeve of the black hoodie they had given her to wipe at her greasy lips. "Great story."

"Look!" Minor whipped himself up, seeing his point had not been communicated. "I been hangin' with some of the Major's guys. They got some of their own scuttlebutt about these things. Seems like when the little ones get in you, their bite got something like a hallucinogenic quality to them when they dig in, a mellow too; sorta like mesc, the real stuff, not the watered-down LSD. So, your pal, Dan, likely didn't feel a thing when it was...uh...happening."

She wasn't sure if the words made her feel any better, but she appreciated the effort, particularly from the guy whose poster she had hanging on her bedroom wall all through her teenaged years. "Thanks, it means a lot," she said. "What was it *Rolling Stones* called you?"

Minor rubbed at his stubbled chin and smiled. "That rag referred to me as the Lullaby King."

"Well, Lullaby King--"

"It wasn't a compliment, ya know?"

Sue smiled. "Well, your Highness," she said, bowing a bit, "I'll be ship-shape when this thing...pulls up? Surfaces? You know. I keep wondering if this strange thing is a giant speed boat or a submarine."

Minor winked. "Neither, love," he said, holding out a hand. "It's a hovercraft; come see."

If one was standing still, Sue surmised, the air temperature would have been blistering. They were heading south, toward the center of the Gulf. The unnamed vessel rode its own pocket of air, ricocheting distantly off of the relatively tame waveforms. It was as though she and Minor stood at the narrow rail atop a tall building in the middle of the sea, parting undulations like Moses on the back of a chariot.

"Headquarters," Minor yelled over the hiss of the air jets, "is on an oil rig out in the middle of the Gulf, I'm told."

They were a flat rock thrown by King Kong, skipping the waves endlessly. For the size of the vessel--forty-foot at best--it clipped at a pretty good pace. And smooth, too. Only the continual salting of her lips told Sue how close the dark little ship came to the gentle Gulf rollers.

"If you get sea sick, you shouldn't stare at those waves for too long." Minor had to yell over the cushioning jets. He turned away from the rolling sea.

Sue grinned. "Like you?" she yelled.

Minor fled below deck, clutching at his straw fedora.

Sue normally felt a little off when out on the water. Apparently, a lift on a hovercraft was a different sort of ride. She gazed out brazenly at the long, smooth undulations like a slow parade of elephants marching under a slate tarpaulin, leviathans trapped beneath denim.

Then, out there, riding on the stitched pocket of a lazy wave was a smudge, a carcinoma on a rolling humpback.

Sue peered out into the glare of the lowering sky above the hypnotizing waves. "What the...?"

Where ancient vessels hosted a crow's nest this ship of the future harbored a harvest of spinning steel rods and cones of black metal lattice; satellite and infrared and smell-o-vision, Sue guessed. But still, a man, locked into an unmoving deck chair, was posted to watch like the youngest deckhand on a whaling ship.

"What's that?" she yelled to him over the ceaseless hiss.

He cupped a hand to his ear. Silly to think her voice would carry. She pointed vehemently out at the object on the rolling horizon.

The watchman squinted and lifted a set of binoculars to his eyes. He was quick to get the mic of his com to his lips to report the object to the bridge.

Sue looked at the field of mutant antenna sprouting from the scalp of the ship like hair plugs for robots.

Surely they already know, she thought.

Cuban refugees, or, that was their story. A cadre of five, now huddling in the already cramped confines of the nameless vessel's bridge. One was a woman. Somehow that made it stink all the worse. And, Sue wondered to herself, does one still have to defect from Cuba?

The answer surprised her a bit.

"What makes you think they were heading for America?" the Major said. "Cuban citizens are still launching rafts, more than ever, now that normalization has not equaled the economic windfall every taxi driver and boxer hoped it would be. And, normalization with the government meant an end to hardship Visas for refugees. They're still Cubans on rafts, but they're not heading to our shores. Mexico or any Caribbean shores where one might work as a busboy in an all inclusive resort are the likely landing spots these days."

Sue leaned in, keeping an eye on the five that had been pulled from the raft. "So," she said, "you believe them?"

"Fuck no," the Major retorted in a whispering growl. "Just look at 'em."

Below the army surplus blankets that had been issued them, they bore long shirts that reminded Sue of British military gear, what she believed they called moisture wicking. A high tech version of wool that kept one warm while allowing sweat to escape. Their long, thick shirts matched, all blacks and dark greens as though a softball team lost at sea, or a platoon.

"What are you going to do?" Minor whispered.

"Let them finish their tea," the Major said. "We're not animals."

Sue and Minor eyed him.

The Major shrugged. "We have ways."

But the Cubans had other ideas.

Just as the Major offered an ambiguous nod to no particular BioFlouretic agent and said the words 'Better Get Out The Cookies' as though he was Neil Armstrong announcing that the Eagle Has Landed, the refugees at each end of the row of five stood up, too short to worry about the tight confines. Attention swept their way and that's when the next two from each end leapt up and swept the bridge with volleys from sidearms they had been hiding in their waistbands. Not usual weapons, some foreign governments' version of the Flouretic hardware, these guns sprayed the Major, Minor and their available staff with bright, yellow pellets.

Sue was knocked back into her private quarters. She hunched there, keeping her head down and covering herself with shaky hands.

Outside her room, the sound of heavy collisions shook the bulkheads. The floor below her vibrated from the contest of giants.

Then there was silence.

Finally, "Where's the old woman?"

The question got answered quickly, and the old woman was summarily dragged out into the command center. Of the original hybrid crew--tech noir agents and daq-runners--only the Major was in attendance, sitting on the floor looking a little touched up.

"Where's everyone else?" Sue demanded.

"Easy, Momma," said one of the supposed refugees. "We just want to talk."

"What are you guys, pirates?"

Three of them were below. One furiously worked the controls while the leader, a squat man with a barbwire scar tracing his jaw, stood over the Major.

"As a matter of fact," he said, giving Sue a lopsided, big-bad-wolf grin. The scar shimmered. "You could say that we are pirates, but we'd be happy to leave once we get what we came for."

Sue looked at the Major. "You?" she asked. "They're here for you?"

More wolfish laughter.

The Major spat red on a dark bulkhead. "No," he said, "these guys don't even know who I am. Nobody does."

"Oh, we know who you are, sweetheart," long scar said, his tone lined with some sort of hispanic flavor. The Major eyed him, doubtfully. "You are the raisin in my oatmeal, ain't he, Tex?" He slapped the other broad shouldered man, another supposed Cuban.

"Hey!" said his compatriot, who hosted a dark, untrimmed beard. "Didn't you guys hear, there are no more Cuban refugees. Obama normalized our asses."

"So, you are Cubans?" Sue asked.

Scrabble beard considered. "We are…"

"Opportunists," Scar finished.

"Pirates," the Major said. "You had it right the first time."

"You know who they are?" Sue asked.

The Major scanned the Cubans. "We know each other," he said.

The pirate trying to work the hovercraft controls spun to face his partners. "It's a no go," he said.

Scar nodded. "Then we're on a time limit." He leaned into the Major. "Hey, Major Raisin, you could give us some more time."

"Why would I do that?"

"Well," Scar said, "not so many places to put folk on this rig. This here floating dock is losing what little altitude it got, and we had to get, shall we say, imaginative with your crew?"

"Show me," Sue said.

"No, hold on, momma…"

But Sue ran past them, which only served to give the interlopers the giggles as though a puppy had run between their legs.

Up on the deck, the problem became clear. The seas had flattened but the horizon moved all the same as the hover jets lost their enthusiasm. Sue realized the dark vessel refused to work for the Cubans. They were going down. The Cubans knew it, including the few that were up on the deck, but they didn't seem too interested in being delivered back into the Gulf. Instead, they looked over the edge of the chock line at something below the ship, where Sue could not see. Sue tumbled toward the rail and looked down into dark waters, growing ever closer.

Dangling from a webwork of bungy lines were the remaining BioFlouretic agents and the Minor crew, hip deep into the Gulf of Mexico, being steeped into the dark water as the hover jets cut in and out.

"Get them up!" Sue bellowed above the intermittent hiss of the failing engines.

The Cubans laughed. She spied the king of somnambulant chord progressions, Darren Minor, flung in and out of the sea like a cheap tea bag in someone's everyday China cup.

Sue pointed ferociously at her rock hero. "Get them up!"

A knowing smile beneath his dark beard bristled, but nothing more.

Sue retreated to the command center.

They had been giving the Major another go when she entered, but they backed off when they noticed her.

"Hey, momma," Scar said, rubbing at abused knuckles. "Get the picture. See what's at stake?"

Sue bent over the Major, his face swollen and bloodied. "You okay?"

He nodded.

That's when Scar grabbed Sue, hard, by the upper arm.

"Thanks for bringing her, Major," he said. "It's a pretty sure thing, you won't let this one go over."

The leader of the high tech pirates tightened his grip on Sue's arm. She winced.

"Let her go," the Major said. "She's got nothing to do with this. She's just a know-nothing civilian."

Sue winced again but this time at the Major's comment; it hurt. Really though, what did she know? She did not even really know the large black man.

Scar chuckled a bit. "You didn't say one word when I put those men over the side," he said. "I think I got you on this one, Major."

"You *do* know each other," Sue said.

"Indeed we do, momma," Scar said. "And what else does the Major know? He's lost this one and we get what we want."

"If it's not the ship, then what is it? You want Darren Minor to sign a copy of *Tales From The Mosquito Coast*?"

The scrabble-bearded associate's eyes bulged. "Damn straight! Yo, Pocco, you remember that time, down on the Terrace, sipping daiquiris---"

"Perro!"

But it was too late, Pocco had been enticed to ponder sipping daiquiris with his mate. The poorly manscaped Perro, down on some sunset-splashed place down by the rim of the very Gulf now threatening to swallow them. An understated A minor chord accompanying their doom.

The Major, one part possum, leapt up and kicked at a throttle knob.

The ship lurched violently to one side. The Cubans fell. The Major had not been bound. He rode the rapid swaying of the deck and grabbed Sue. He hit a button on the bulkhead above them and a big breathing mask fell. He wrapped it around her face, and with another button, caused it to suck tight onto her, making her lips pucker.

They hit hard, and as the water poured in from the open hatch, a cool atmosphere fed into the helmet.

Sue was underwater before she knew it. The Major swam about, holding a great gulp of air in his massive chest. He swam out the hatches to where his men were, Sue presumed. The Cubans floated like poorly kept goldfish.

As if by some signal, and why doubt that it was, the vessel's hatches locked down, and the streams of bubbles, like the powerful aerators in the eel tanks, rushed into the cabin. The space was pressurized in a moment. Sue removed the face mask. The water-logged Cubans were out. A flashing red button near a flat screen monitor attracted Sue's attention. She hit the button and the Major appeared on the screen. Face masks like the one that kept Sue alive snaked out of every point on the deck of the hovercraft, now surfacing and bobbing on the waves. It was these external masks that allowed those on the outside--including the Major--breath while the unnamed vessel dove beneath the waves.

The Major removed his mask. "Sue!" he cried into the camera mic. "Hit the green button now!"

She did. The hatches opened and the Major returned.

Here's what they were after.

The Cubans lay, completely secured and heavily monitored, on the floor.

The Major snapped the locks on the sturdy travel case and opened the lid. Nestled in thick egg crate foam were two slender jars. In each jar a pregnant sliver of black shivered.

"The eels?" Sue asked.

"Whatever they are," the Major said.

"You really don't know what they are?"

"No," said the Major, "that's for the scientists. My realm is training agents on these crazy weapons the company made and how to use them to stop these things."

"You make it seem like the company exists because of these things."

The Major shrugged. "These and others."

Sue's heart skipped a beat. "Others?"

The Major did not respond directly to the question, only staring down into the captive black squiggles. "They're not Cubans, not really, whatever their ethnic origins."

"What are they? For that matter, what are you?"

The Major gave one of the jars a jiggle. Sue was too tired to react. The Major showed his own weariness. "Where there are gaps, there we are, buffers, linkages between eras, tethering philosophy to necessity."

"Where do these things come into play, the creatures?"

"They exist," the Major said. "These things *are* and they *are* bad. We *are* and we *must* be. There aren't other options, just survival."

"We?" Sue asked. "We are threatened by these? All of us?"

The Major walked one of the jars over to where one of the 'Cubans' sat, Scarface sutured to a compatriot with self-locking, nylon cable ties. The Major looked through the clear canister, eyeing the shiny scar. "Things happen."

Sue dropped her chin to her chest. How could anyone consider that a satisfying response? Even a man?

Sensing Sue's chagrin, the large black man smiled and put away the jar of black, oily death. "I don't make them, Sue. I don't know who does; God, maybe? I just ask that I'm given the tools to do the job, in this case, stop these things from getting loose."

"The plant back there, across from Minor Mansions?"

"Scientists are in charge here," the Major said. "This unit is unique in that they answer, solely, to a consortium of scientists, folks largely ignored. We were given to them, muscle to get the job done where needed."

"Probably not destroying factories contributing to global warming?"

The Major chuckled. "Far more direct threats. Stuff the public would understand even less than the effects of cow farts on global temperatures but require immediate reaction."

Sue nodded at the captives. "And these guys?"

"First layer of misinformation," the Major said, glaring into the clear canister holding a little monster. "They thought these things are some kind of weapon they can sell on the dark market."

"And these things are not weapons?" Sue asked. "You're sure?"

The Major seemed to consider a response as he quietly closed the armored travel case. "If they're weapons," he said, "then they are the nameless, constant threat of nature against us, against all people, a return to the basic struggle of early man--the feeling that the planet is working against our existence. These things were not made. They were always here."

NINE

It started as a dot, dipping below the horizon, then reasserting itself where the scientists lived, the supposed head of this operation. Some long minutes later, moments that threatened both heart-rending threat and endless anticipation, Sue could see it, set against the dying sun, a tall bit of technology sprouting out of the sea.

The sun went down and a deep lethargy settled into Sue. She stumbled down to the lone set of quarters and was out as soon as her head hit the bulb of foam, a pillow built directly into the bunk mattress.

Sue dreamed of a rock concert. The opening act sucked. It was a bunch of slimy eels playing horns, but instead of blowing into them, they sucked at the mouth pieces until a mighty tide pulled at the confused crowd. Sue felt herself lift from the ground, on the way to the shiny bell of a tuba hooked onto a slimy bit of black wriggling excitedly on the nipple mouthpiece. She thought to scream but could not remember how. She flew, but a hand caught her. She turned from the stage to tell the person holding her back not to let go.

It was Dan Nickle. "Don't worry, darlin'" he said, calmly. "I won't ever let you go."

Which was nice, but it was funny. She never really said it out loud: *don't let go.*

"The existing species that is the appropriate analog would not be anything in the eel family, but something from the snail group."

Sue sighed. "Just tell me there's an end to this."

She was short and solid and Asian, and she was a scientist. Except for a few loose agents, all the staff members wandering about were scientists, and young.

In fact, Sue, in her depleted state, wandered the comparatively expansive walkways and workstations of the deep sea rig, feeling assaulted by the millennial propensity toward protest.

"This is all because of politicians' need to reassure the SUV purchasing public that their need for overindulgence will not be threatened."

"If you build a house with vampires, be prepared to see some dark stuff sucked from weird places."

"You're a child of the 60's, you understand."

Sue may have raised a hand to protest. "Actually, I…"

They did not care. Their stylishly-thick framed glasses defined how they saw the world.

When Sue finally felt stationary, among a group that did not replenish itself with new faces, she asked the key question. "But, what are they?"

The solidly built Asian woman answered unabashedly. "We're not sure."

Sue threw her hands in the air. "That's it. I'm done. When's the next hovercraft home?"

A gentle hand rested on her forearm. It belonged to a particularly small person with hair shaved close above each ear. Sue found it difficult to say what gender this person was. "We know far more now," gender neutral said, soothingly, "but a scientist who's asked to be definitive without a proper period of observation and experimentation can be slippery…"

"Like an eel?" Sue asked.

The rather sweet, gender unspecific dwarf smiled. "Yes, exactly."

"But they're not eels," stout and Asian said. "Of that we're sure."

They seemed to be happy to have an audience.

Sue shook her head. "Let's back up," she said. "I'm Sue Mayfield." She stuck out her hand, not sure if people even still shook hands.

"Dr. Andrea Barnabas," solid Asian said.

"Dr. Ruth Brahmanhamnstans," no longer gender neutered, short woman said.

"You two a couple or something?" Sue found herself saying, spontaneously regretful.

The two scientists smiled knowingly at each other.

Sue smirked. "Is that a more difficult question to answer than anything about the eels?"

"Entities," Andrea corrected.

"Entities," Sue echoed. "And you can't tell me anything about them?"

Ruth sprung onto tip-toes. "Oh!" She exclaimed. "The data is endless. The traits identified, nearly so."

"And then there is apocrypha," Andrea said. "Stories, lots of stories." She added at Sue's apparent confusion.

Sue eyed a collection of open space conference areas more akin to a rumpus room in the Playboy mansion. She sat down heavily on an overstuffed leather lounger. The young scientists followed her like baby ducks. "Like what?" Sue asked. "Regale me with tales of horror and woe. Don't get upset if I pass out."

Dr. Andrea Barnabas took a deep breath. "Well…"

***

It was a gusher, an orgasm of pure black, bodily oils of antediluvian creatures distilled and simmered deep in mother earth's womb, a placenta of igneous mantle enveloping whole species and rebirthing them as combustible fuels for all-terrain vehicles and leaf blowers, diesel cranes and mopeds. The crew working for Clearonics Oil must have thought they hit their payday, their ship had come in, the ship taking them off this rig and onto easy street.

But they didn't know a few strips of black death had snuck into the rivulets of black gold.

There weren't many of those first ones, and the shift was something just short of a skeleton crew.

When the first of them went down, it appeared that scant wildcatters running the rig must have been self mutilating by injecting themselves directly with the crude oil itself. To those men (Brazilians), the infestation was a complete mystery.

One morning they happily sat around the breakfast table then a man started acting strange. By dinner two of them blossomed into fountains of deadly black squiggles. The last man in the morning hung himself.

Sometime in the night they had called the Coast Guard, but it was too late. They were all the walking dead, birthing chambers for more entities that seemed to be part of the gusher. And, they were right, because the pocket they had tapped into housed both the crude and the slumbering things, a creature so bent on survival, it reconstructed itself from bit pieces, the most fundamental form of itself.

Then the company supply ship brought precious cargo, a rescue team.

That was Jimmy Corbett's team. The rig scientists who sat down with Sue knew him. Jimmy was ex-SEAL, as capable a leader as ever filled out a pair of fatigue pants.

The first night on the rig, Jimmy's private little commando crew discovered these things' dirty little secret.

They can be sneaky when they want, darn sneaky. And, they have this really sneaky, slimy capability.

"Their bite delivers a dose of hallucinogen?" Sue asked.

Not a bite, really, the scientists explained (one a product of Harvard, the other of MIT), really more a violently invasive form of diffusion, the small ones slip in on a molecular level.

Poor Jimmy was the first afflicted. The things were basically loose on the station when the rescue team settled into place, hiding and waiting. The rig was lifeless when the muscle men with big guns climbed aboard. Who knows what they made of that, but it was likely they did not perceive a threat.

The security video must have given them a clue, but our slimy little friends have many tricks.

Jimmy rose in the night out of a bad dream.

Security cameras were (still are) in all the quarters. Corporate owners of this rig run toward the paranoid end of the spectrum.

Jimmy got himself up out of bed and loaded his sidearm. He never really woke from the bad dreams, it had simply morphed into a bad trip.

He started with those that were asleep. God knows what paranoid delusion the worms had induced within him. He sprayed the brains of the sleeping all over the bulkheads. The shootout that occurred with the SEALS who were awake and on duty only served to spread the bloody macro viruses around the rig.

Jimmy had it best, the scientists telling the story figured; he didn't know he was dying.

***

"And then what?" Sue tried to ask as the two scientists were called away.

The staff's regular pace seemed to be a gear just short of beehive. Without company, Sue found it hard to stay in the land of the living. A hand shook her awake.

"Hey!"

It was not a polite emergence into reality, but like a lot of life, it was what it was.

And these days, it was about survival.

Jimmy never really woke from the bad dream.

Sue's exhaustion made it difficult to account for all the folks working on the rig, but she was sure this man was new to her. He was the shape of an earthen jar if the jar was built to hold melted lead. In his rumpled polo, this man--a young man to Sue despite the grey at both closely cropped temples--stood out in every way from the ant colony of young hipster scientists in their white coats and Doc Martens.

"Hey," he repeated. "This is no place to sleep. Have they issued you quarters?"

Sue shook away the cobwebs. "No," she said. "I guess I passed out not long after arriving."

"You can't stay here," he said, sad brown eyes behind thick glasses. His face was dark with a multi-day bristle. "Heavy equipment moving through here soon, and, like lots of stuff around here, dangerous."

Somehow, she was comforted by the wrinkled collar of his polo he'd decided to stretch over several days.

Sue offered a shaky hand. He took it and hoisted her up off the open space couch. "I'm Sue."

"Mike Stewart," he said. He was strong. A human wall that could, without question, Hercules-style, support that weight of the world, if asked.

80

She leaned heavily on Mike Stewart and felt, instantly, good about doing so.

"They," she said, feeling, automatically like Stewart would understand she referred to the young female scientists, "told me there had been a lots of folks, teams, that had come and gone here."

Mike shook his round head. "I'm just an operations tech asked to work above his paygrade," he said. "But, ironically, because I'm not encumbered with degrees from various ivy leagues, I come cheap, and tend to out-last the latest rotation of former Yale sorority chicks gone wild. Sorry if I offend."

Clearly he was not sorry, but given the circumstance, survival weighed somewhere above politically sensitive affect.

"I'm not in charge," he said, "not nearly, but if I had some general advice, I'd say, listen to all the varying opinions you're gonna get hit with and pick your favorite. One is as good as another. No one here really knows what they're up against."

Sue coughed. A large chunk of phlegm came up that she suppressed. "I'm not a scientist."

Mike shouldered her weight. "Well," he said, "even if you're from the corporate, or, God-forbid, from some senator's office, the advice remains the same--keep your pretty little head down."

Sue smiled half way to a near collapse, almost coming to in Stewart's armpit. "I'm none of those things," she said. "I'm the neighbor."

Through his Buddha reassurance, Sue sensed a portion of Stewart's crumpled collar disbelief that he did not vocalize. "Sleep can only help."

There was a room. It was dark and separate from the rest of the working parts of the rig. "This is you," he said, "a shift of shut eye   can't   hurt,   whoever   you   are."
Then Sue considered. For these parts, her grey hair only could mean oversight from the great and far-away place that they called BioFlouretic homebase or this Consortium. They saw her age and felt the weight of accountability.

"They don't know what they're doing," she said, already feeling the tentacles of a deep sleep grab for her. "They don't even know what those things are."

Stewart stood in the doorway, blocking most of the light from the hallway. "Worse than that," his wide outline said. "These folks are the only thing keeping the gates of hell from swinging wide open and releasing these slimy little demons on the whole world. You should see the computer projections. Not pretty."

Not pretty.

The words followed Sue into her dreams.

***

Her youngest daughter is five years old and does not want Sue to touch her as she tries to ride her bike.

"No mommy! I can do it."

"But dear," Sue said, sure she was the reasonable one in this circumstance. After all, she was not the five year old trying to teach herself how to ride a bike. "We have to get this done so I can wake up. If this becomes a nightmare, I'll wake up and kill everyone else on the base."

The youngest daughter whose name should be known to Sue, even in a dream--

but was not accessible--kept one, oversized-sneaker on a peddle while she looked directly into her mother's eyes. "But, Mommy," she said, from underneath the awkward weight of the floral helmet, "everyone else is already dead. The dream eels got them in their sleep."

Sue woke with a gasp, a light sweat peppering her forehead. A lightning flash lit the hallway outside the doorless hatch. The hallway was empty, and she was sure the dream version of Patsy had delivered to her from an episode thirty-four years distant some bit of foresight onto her ancient, wayfaring mother.

Then someone walked by the open hatchway. Sue felt better, but not much.

You should see the computer projections.

"Maybe I should," she said to the room, and hoisted herself up out of bed.

***

The storm outside raged. The rig did not move much, despite the angry wind whipping the hull. It was some minutes before Sue ran into anyone.

When Mike Stewart entered the room, both he and Sue jumped. A lightning flash, closely followed by its thundering shadow, added a degree of melodrama to the scene, the two adults caught in mid cower. They laughed.

"No sleep for me these days," Stewart said. "I'm the last of the tech team. These white coats may know indigenous species and tectonic plates, the cretaceous period and red tides, but they couldn't run a virus scan or a clean update to save their lives. And this place lives and dies on its network."

They were in the common area again, big windows trickled with Gulf rain. "This is a pretty big place," she said, sitting heavily on a couch of black leather. "Ten pounds of science in a five pound bag. They must use computers to...wipe their hinies."

The big man laughed. "Too true. Maintaining the satellite hook up alone is like bailing out the Titanic with a shot glass."

"But there's only one of you? The shadow group running this operation can't afford a larger support team?"

"It isn't that."

Sue sighed and stretched out on the couch. Distant thunder rumbled. "What happened to them, Mike?"

"The same thing that happens to everyone around here," he said. "They don't know what those things are, not really, so containment is...an issue."

Sue remembered the demonstration gone wrong back in Clearwater. The big creatures breaking their tank like a burst aneurism.

"Why do you stay?" Sue asked, almost afraid to hear the answer.

The big tech shrugged and adjusted the waistline of his shorts around his global stomach. "When you see what's going on here, really going on, you'll see. Giving up is not an option."

Sue pulled down hard on her drooping jowls. "Pretty sure I don't know what you're talking about. Pretty sure I don't want to be here, but I guess Alice was ready to go home soon after a dodo bird talked to her."

"I shouldn't sit." But he sat, his muscular bulk relaxing for just a moment. He pulled himself upright. "They, these kids, constantly convince themselves they got their hands around the limits of these things. First it was lead shielding, then it was glass tubing. Now, the eggheads running the joint are sliding all their chips onto hexiglass cylinders, either with a nine volt protective current or a 120 amp containing force, or something. It all adds up to the same thing."

"What's that?"

"Mysticism," he said, "wishful thinking. They have no idea."

"Then why stay?"

"Just in case."

"Just in case what?"

A particularly violent eruption of thunder struck seismically through the rig, causing all of the day lights to come on.

"Oops!" Sue said. "Surprise start for everyone."

"Nah," Stewart said. "This is the first shift."

It's not even daylight, Sue almost said. But when you're guarding the gates of hell...

Stewart shrugged. "Gotta go."

He stood and moved toward the next area where a simple update or patch was needed to refill the font of technical holy water known as networking and computing. He was quickly replaced by somnambulant bodies still in boxer shorts, girls particularly, in zombie crawl for caffeine. Sue missed him immediately.

These were open space workers. They settled on the couches with more ease than Sue's generation would have been gathering at the diner lunch counter before work.

It was when one of them--there seemed so many curvy young women here--extracted from some inner recess of her morning robe a long tube with a living specimen of one of the squiggly demons in it that Sue tensed.

"Don't play with that," she said.

The young woman sucked deeply at the edge of her broad coffee mug. "We don't play, " she said, "who are you?"

Dr. Barnabas joined her colleague, carrying a plate of fruit and eggs back from the pre-prepared breakfast bar.

Sue did not know how to respond to the young scientist, ignoring her. "Mike was just here," Sue said.

"He doesn't like these things."

The female scientists in the boy boxers passed a vial back and forth. "For good reason," the unknown scientist said.

Ruth Brahmanstans proffered the vial, turning it in her fingers and peering inside. "Nasty things."

The creature inside jerked in its liquid coffin.

Sue jerked too. She leapt off the sofa.

Ruth pulled her down. "Easy, gal," she said. "Nothing to worry about. It can't possibly get out of that container."

"People, scientists like you, keep telling me that," Sue said. "Then they die."

The scientist waved Sue off. "Pssh," she said. "These things are all over this rig anyway, in various containers of one sort or another. Either this thing is safe to be around or nothing is."

Barnabas got up to get herself more coffee. She let the container of death drop recklessly on the dark cushions. Ruth was between Sue and the creature. This did not ease Sue's mind much.

Ruth didn't seem to mind. She did not even look at the vial. Sue stayed on the couch for pride's sake, but as far she could get from the thermos sized container. She teetered on one butt cheek on the lip of the far cushion.

There was nowhere to go. The slimy creature just a few butt cheeks away in the not-too-secure looking mason jar, figured as the devil she knew, but Sue could be sure the bulkheads around her hid hellish hosts of the little demons, subjects in ongoing experiments to kill off the ultimate invasive species.

A distant dampness at her hip caused Sue to jump a bit. Someone had been careless with their coffee on the thick cushions that caved in at the assault of average adult weight, causing the instability of both coffee drinkers and their java. Not practical, really, Sue thought.

Sue checked the damp spot to make sure it wasn't an eel thing. Then wiped at the spot. Part of her told her to get up, but some exhausted sense of pride kept her to her seat.

A wet tickle and she wiped. She checked and there was only a trickle of mocha.

A giant wall of olive drab muscled in from a distant hatch, grabbed a chair and dragged it over to the couch, spun the chair to sit backwards on it, and sat facing Sue. It was the Major.

"This place is fucked," he announced.

Sue could not consider a scenario that spun the edifice of authority that was the Major into whiny restlessness. "No Cubans to battle?" Sue asked, amused.

The Major clicked his tongue with middle school disdain, but checked the room before he responded, putting the flat of his hand up against his mouth for presumed discretion. "These college chicks don't know what the hell they're doing," he said. "They don't. This place is a powderkeg. They got thousands of the things in all these shiny containers they want to call safe."

Sue nodded. "Whistling in the dark."

"Hell, whistling with a muzzle stuck in their faces," he said. He looked away darkly. "And they took the Cubans away from me."

No truculent child had ever regretted the loss of a toy more. With another click of his tongue, the Major got up and left the common room.

Sue reached out to him, about to offer condolences when the wet kiss at her hip tapped her more urgently.

Sue slapped at the feeling and caught herself knocking away the seeking skolex of an eel thing. It got loose.

She screamed, standing and slapped at herself.

A dark slip of nightmare launched itself from the cushy leather couch toward every line in Sue's seventy-year-old face. Doctor Ruth Brahmanhamnstans caught the enlivened

exclamation point in mid assault. But, now, Doctor Ruth grimaced, and, the stopping fist that had saved Sue, shook with convulsive intensity until the fist itself shattered into a parade of black slivers, hungrily seeking hosts.

Sue fell back, lost in a revelry of hopes lost, expectations blown.

The inflicted woman grunted, clenching her entire being against what was about to happen. The grunt grew to growl. She shook all over.

I don't have to watch this, Sue told herself. But she saw it anyway.

Brahmanhamnstans balled herself up around the fist, still growling. Her large, round shoulder seemed to take over most of her body, hiding her face and the fist at the center of her. The growl became a wail.

Sue told herself to back away, and while she failed at this, she was shocked to see the other scientists leaning into the wailing woman, hands going out to the big shaking shoulders.

How long have these women played with these things, Sue wondered. *Why aren't they running to the hills? Why aren't I?*

Maybe--even as the already large shoulders began inflating with subcutaneous infestation--the other scientists, Ruth's friends still had hope that the worst was not about to happen.

How many times had she worked at herself to convince her subconscious that hope rest around every corner.

Sure, it was her idea to sell her house and move into assisted living facility. Sure, when pressed, she, originally a mild mannered Minnesotan, surfed the dark network younger folk swam in called the internet and discovered a place called Minor Mansions, and, oh how young that felt. Choose your own iceberg. But she did not know anyone in Florida, only had the hope that other daq-heads might converge, and by their own coke-fueled recollection (Sue never partook herself), conjured up for all the residents some sense of youth and vitality, circa 1972.

But, in the end, she had been abandoned as anyone else in The Mansions. She had not seen any of her family in three years. In fact, the kitsch of the yacht-rock premise lulled Sue's kids into spreading to their progeny that grandma was living the 'Me' generation's version of the American Dream, to rock on, to drink on, to die as soon as possible of all other rock-n-roll options.

Except Sue was not much of a risk taker, which made her something of a mediocre daq-head. Adventure, to a young, college-aged Sue meant a joint when offered, beer as invited, and good grades at St. Paul's with hope of achieving a corporate position in accordance with a college degree. At AT&T, that meant another eight-hundred dollars a year compared to all of

Sue's associates in the company. Ironically, answering customer calls had nothing to do with her degree in communications.

So, Sue might be willing to admit she was out of her depth when dealing with the present threat. She would confess that this late life adventure into high risk was regrettable. But, she was not the one, degree or otherwise, reckless or not, with a squiggly, black demon crawling through her.

The big shoulders slumped as Ruth's arms fell out of their sockets where the sockets had been eaten through by the smallest version of the super eels. The arms, encased in worms, splatted to the floor. The shoulders slumped and the comforting hands retracted.

Ruth's scream silenced as her head hosed the other scientists with worms.

The killer eel from the jar was on the loose. From one scientist first, the thing gained position on everyone else in the lounge, digging deeply into well-educated girl flesh, to fester, multiply, and launch from one host to another.

To further prove the folly of staff working this rig, responders piled into the common room rather than opening exits and commanding the as-yet unafflicted to flee the scene.

They have a hallucinogenic bite, Sue reminded herself when she saw a young woman doctor in comfy sweats explode, geysering forth a dark spume of super leeches. A safety responder grabbed for the armless body--still standing--but he only served to jostle the head loose. Then he was overtaken by satanic paisleys.

Sue was bumped hard on one bony hip and sent reeling while the young women, forgetting their callous attitude toward their deadly bounty, pranced and screamed like nine-year-olds having traversed a tunnel of spiderwebs in the dark. But they were big, large, swinging well-toned hips hewn from sugary ice lattes and make your own sundae night on the rig, no doubt. Sue bobbed on the waves of their panic before sinking down, sure hip surgery, if she escaped hosting a demonic worm, lay in her near future.

A full-figured hip knocked her into a dagger elbow which flung her onto a hefty set of boobs from which Sue trampolined into someone's arms. This person, hoisting from under her arms, simply lifted her from the room, heels dragging.

They were out of the common room to parts unknown. For all Sue knew, there were only worse nightmares pocketed within the belly of the rig. She and her dragger left the big room of hysteria, but Sue felt sure she had one in her, somewhere, squirming silently, unseen like cancer metastasized into animal form.

She felt sure of the infestation when she heard music, guitar music, from the direction of her rescue. It was someone who could really play. It was good. It was sweet, and she did not trust how good it made her feel. The bite of the sickly entity had a hallucinogenic effect, incapacitating the host while the invader quickly devoured tissue, turning the poor soul into an incubator for more unspeakable slivers of black death.

But the music grew and it surrounded her. She gave into the madness and sang along. Her brain would not allow Sue to name the song, but she knew it. And something more…

The author of the song was on the rig too. It was a Darren Minor song.

As Sue had expected, she was not being brought to a place as wide and airy and Apple think-tank as the common room, but it looked safer and her savior locked a very heavy hatch behind them as they entered what appeared to be a grungy cafeteria, mostly forgotten by the millennials who had turned the comfy common room into a coffee house.

Someone who worked here brought a guitar and the king of yacht rock managed to get his gnarled but practiced hands on its well-polished neck.

Sue turned. Her saviour had been Mike Stewart. He smiled and winked at her. And though she was sure he was not a fan, he sang along.

There are some who like their workin'…

Sue stood, surveying the gathering. The Major was here. He tapped his thick fingers on a calcite table top. Tables were long, food presumably served family style.

He shrugged. "I put in a request for *Welcome to The TerrorDome*," he said. "Pretty sure it's next."

Folks we know struggle and strife

Mike Stewart, thick fingers hooked carelessly in belt loops (as if he had not just seen the death of all his coworkers) crooked his ear and tapped a sneakered foot to the rhythm of the gentle chords on the Fender acoustic. "It ain't Chick Corea, but it will do."

Say to me you failed to make a livin'...

Now, Sue was convinced that it was over. Not that they were all waiting here in this pocket of safety for their doom, to be run through with unstoppable creatures from a bygone age, but they were already dead. The toxic bite of the creature on the common room couch sent Sue into a state of complete delusion.

Or, maybe, she was already dead. This was a kind of purgatory where the victims of creatures, perhaps a few of many more to come, waited in a sort of dentist's waiting room, complete with calming music from the master snake charmer himself, the Pied Piper that had drawn Sue out of her own house (having settled down in Ohio) of forty years to come live in the gecko infested humidity of Florida's west coast.

At least I'll live the rest of my life...

Minor's fingers let go most of the strings, allowing a C chord to resolve into something else in the C family but strummed upwardly, most of the high strings played open, sounding something like church bells.

Sue applauded; why not, she was dead, wasn't she? She might as well enjoy it. No one else clapped.

They all gave her a rather curious look.

Somewhere outside the thick bulkheads of the small cafeteria, a low booming throbbed through the plate steel structure.

Mike Stewart, the plain spoken computer engineer, was there. Minor and a couple of his crew were there. The Major and what looked like a sole member of his BioFlouretic security firm managed to find their way to this spot just as the trouble began.

Adding to the dreamy quality of the scene were the Cubans. They were all there, intact and, except for a few scrapes applied by The Major on the boat, seemed in good health.

None of them were smiling at the rare treat of a personal serenade by one of the top earning musicians of the last thirty years. It was not a room of mirth after all.

Sue shook her head a bit. "So," she said. "I'm not dead?"

Stewart reached out, lifted her sleeve, and in revealing a dark and newly hatched bruise, gave it a merciless poke.

"Oww!" Sue yelped.

"Sorry," Mike said, "not for the poke, but the disappointment. You're very much alive. We're all alive, probably the only ones. And, we're all very much screwed."

TEN

Sue had long given up on getting to the bottom of all this. She had been teased by near death more times than an old woman should. But, the big men in the room must have come to an understanding. All cards were on the table if they wanted to get out of this alive.

And there was the rest of the world to consider.

In the absence of any other rig workers (the hatch cutting them off from the slaughter eerily silent), Mike Stewart had to stand in as an expert on both the workings of the rig and the properties of their destroyer.

His great round shoulders held high in full shrug, he almost had to laugh. "Here's what I do: debugging operating systems," he said, "not de-slugging fortresses to scientific failure; that's not me."

"But you were here at the hub," Darren Minor said.

"Didn't you tour with the Grateful Dead in '72?" Stewart asked.

"1976, but yes."

"Could you play their entire set?"

"No," Minor said, "but I sat in for a few encores."

"Well," Stewart said, "these lady doctors didn't invite me to do anything but ensure satellite transmission and maintain the network firewall."

The Major stood to make a point but was interrupted by a noise from his midsection. "Sorry," he said, "I haven't eaten since I got here. Debriefing these guys." He indicated the refugees that had tried to hijack the hovercraft.

The last of the Minor roadies leapt up and skittered to where Sue guessed a kitchen hid behind the sickly grey bulkhead. "I'll check to see what we have."

The Major nodded. He waved at the roadie absently. "Thanks." Then his attention leveled on Stewart. "But you must have heard something all those months out here with these gals.

Before you determined they'd crossed man meat off their menu, you were, likely, hanging on every word."

Stewart rubbed at his round chin, days of stubble gathering there below mildly tinted glasses. "Well," he said, "I did have to run the video equipment when they recorded their experiments."

Darren Minor snapped his fingers. "That sounds useful."

Sue felt a lump of bile rise in her throat. "I don't think I could take any more gore."

"Then," Stewart said, striding to a control panel embedded in a bulkhead as grey as Mother's Day in Seattle. He punched a few keys and the monitor imprisoned there glowed with life. "You may want to see what they recorded *after* the experiments. They sat down with the camera and vlogged on the trajectory of various theories as more facts became available."

"You upgrade the intel, you upgrade the strategy," the Major announced.

Stewart nodded. "Most of the early stuff is guesswork as useful as anything anyone of us could puke up, but let me see if I can find something more recent."

The Cubans took the cue, each jauntily hoisting a Captain Morgan leg onto a cafeteria stool, settling into the intent position as though their favorite Disney cartoon was on the marquee for this show.

Stewart looked particularly at Sue as he grabbed a remote. "Sorta like confessionals on reality TV," he said. And, seeing Sue had no idea what confessionals were, added something far more helpful. "Not squishy, at all. Helpful, not sure, but no violence."

First up for a face to face with the digital camera was Doctor Andrea Barnabas, specialty completely unknown to Sue.

Mike, she said into the mic. *Are we ready? Double check the gain. The audio is most important. We have to preserve this.*

"Where's her shirt?" Sue asked of the image on the screen.

Whatever Doc Barnabas had been up to, her onscreen persona was stripped down to an old fashioned, lace bra that she overflowed like a Netherlands dike.

"I don't know," one of the Cubans (accent completely gone, seemingly far less Cuban than ever) said. "But she's got my attention."

Sue noted most of the men seemed transfixed which should be because their lives hung in the balance, but she would not bet money on it.

We may have made a breakthrough.

Sue had to look away to take the young, full-figured scientist's message to heart, no matter the stakes. The picture suggested the most likely breakthrough was the well-educated woman's d-cups would escape their lacey bonds.

Sue could hear well enough.

It's just as we thought. Their resistance to penetration through mechanical means indicates multigenerational adaptations to an environment of monumental pressure, far beyond the millibar scale we surface creatures would measure such things by. In other words, it's a good thing we upgraded the BioFlouretic squad to acidic ordinance or they would not have a chance to stop these things from doing exactly as they like.

"Here, here," the Major said.

None of the men seemed to mind that there were bits of black seepage left uncleansed from the supple spots on the well-rounded Dr. Barnabas.

However, such chemical means would not work on a wide scale in that the concentrations we distilled down for our agents' weapons would do as much harm to a populated area as the creatures themselves. We have to put our faith in the radiology results. The physicists among us must prevail!

Now Barnabas looked exasperated.

Oh, and Sonia and her sound wave theory.

Barnabas shook her head sadly and was gone, Grand Canyon cleavage and all.

Stewart slid a finger over a wall-mounted pad, scanning through hours of footage. He let escape a few moments of an experiment where a number of the stout, curvy scientists, hidden beneath layers of protective gear, peered through dark, protective goggles at the contents of a cloudy tank. No sooner did the tank glow bright with some sort of invasive stimulus (science by Zeus), than a critter broke from its bonds and attacked one of its curious tormentors. The tables were turned; the eel creature wriggled all over the black goggles of the nearest scientist, this time to be shot by one of the special acid guns.

More screams, more death. Mike Stewart cut away and cast a guilty glance in Sue's direction.

Next time the video wheel stopped, it landed on a confessional, Brahamnhamnstans, the contrite reporter.

Running low on materials. Not sure we'll make it to the next supply chopper. Seems almost a waste of energies continuing Sonia's work with sonics. But, the DNA results are in and most of us are agreed: we have reconsidered an extraterrestrial origin. Clearly our rig, what was once the Sweetwater, when they had tapped through the rather thin crust here, hit a pocket in the mantle that we had considered to be an anaerobic bubble where these creatures, likely having thrived in the poisonous gases of the many active volcanoes of the Cretaceous, were not buried by the Chicxulub meteor event but rather was delivered to Earth by the 15 kilometer rock, the Great Impactor, the dino killer, when it crashed into the region we now know as the Yucatan...

The image was gone.

Sue turned to Stewart. "What happened?" she asked. "Where's the rest?"

"That's it," he said. "Like the Bra queen said…"

Minor chucked. "The what?"

"She resisted nicknames," Stewart said. "But somewhere about the third time I tried to say, Brahamanhamnstans, I called her the Bra Queen and told her she'd have to accept the moniker or I wouldn't share any more of my illegal torrents of *Game of Thrones*. She wised up. It was a good nickname, both a play on her name and, like a lot of her colleagues, Ruth's cups tended toward overflow."

"Yeah," the Major said, "we get it, they all had huge tits, but how does that help us survive this shit storm?"

Stewart hid behind another shrug of running-back shoulders.

But Sue stepped into him before he could verbalize what the shoulders suggested: *What? Me? I'm just the tech guy!*

"Listen!" She cawed behind a stern mommy finger. "You are either a whole heck of a lot stupider than you look--and I doubt that--or you're holding back. I get it, months on the waterlogged tree fort with nothing but buxom women trading periods has made you, a generally mild-mannered guy, gun shy. But, now is not the time to save people's feeling, 'cause in about an hour, there might not be any people to insult, nor their feelings to save. Get me?"

Stewart was an alright guy. He smiled and considered the tips of his sneakers for a moment. "These things are bad."

Scarface, the 'Cuban', chuckled sourly. "Breaking news!" Sue no longer detected a Spanish flavor to his speech.

"The folks running this place were getting nowhere, fast." Stewart did not lose his subtle, mirthless grin. "But they seemed to have nailed what they were dealing with, and, I thought, had something to work with on a cure. You heard it on the video file--"

"Hey!"

It was the strident rasp of an Ozzy Osbourne scream, but the Minor roadie who delivered it looked happy enough.

"Look what I found!"

He did not appear to find anything. His hands were empty, like Sue's stomach. The Major's stomach growled again to match the predatory grimace on his dark features.

But then someone popped into the dining area from what appeared from Sue's angle to be a rather bare, if not gleaming, kitchen.

It was a young woman and she came bearing gifts; a tray of snacks as long as one of the Major's muscular arms. Sue had no mystic beliefs. She did not believe in such things as clairvoyance. But she was pretty sure she could hear the thoughts of the men around her as they eyed the woman's tray of appetizers, worthy of Thanksgiving preliminaries on Plymouth Rock.

She was almost painfully thin but the almost heady maleness of the room gravitated toward this unidentified woman more than they had transfixed on fleshy spill-over of the other, now dead, denizens of the sea platform that had once drilled for oil when it bore the name *Sweetwater*. She was flat chested, but she had food.

"The video stopped," the young woman said, "because there was no more to say. They had taken their research as far as it would go. Either we'd find the answer, and everyone could claim a piece, ride their own version into a book deal and a permanent post at the Ivy League of their choice. Or, we were all dead, all of us, all life larger than a toad would be wiped out. The stakes have not changed."

She suddenly caught the intensity of the gazes fixed on her and lifted the tray protectively before her. "Oh, and it was wine and cheese night before the inevitable happened. I'm surprised that…"

The men descended and it was all she could do to resist throwing the tray down before them and flee as one would before feral dogs.

She let the tray drop onto a cafeteria table and stepped back.

"Good-googly-goo!" Darren Minor exclaimed. "That's the biggest, most inviting, wedge of Brie I've ever seen."

No venue of vultures ever picked a carcass cleaner than what the large men did to the tray of treats, brie cheese being the greatest of these. Mike Stewart loitered outside of this, like a jackal waiting his turn at the meal. Instead, he took the young woman by the arm and ushered her over to Sue, who, though pretty hungry, could not comprehend penetrating the wall of muscular backs to get her bit of brie, so she lingered at the periphery, hoping for a cracker and a slice of Monterey Jack.

Mike swept a hand before the young woman like Vanna White about to let slip the secrets to the universe, one letter at a time.

"This is Sonia," he said. "And, as far as I can tell, she's the one with the answer to this mess."

"I joined the operation a little late," Sonia said, dipping a cracker into a not too soft wedge of brie cheese. A neighboring green grape rolled loose from her plate and dropped to the bare, steel floor. "But from what I can gather, the Brazilian oil company, PetroLine, broke through to what their sonar readings told them was a large cache of crude somewhere deep in the crust. And, it could be there *was* oil there. No one knows for sure but either in the pocket of oil or just below it was a bubble of other material, some sticky stuff that was unidentifiable, some kind of ooze. That's where these things had been hiding for God-knows-how-long. What I can tell you for sure is that when the supply ship came, there wasn't anything left of the drill team except a mess of ungathered crude all over the decks, some of that sticky stuff, and the clothes of the drill crew."

"The Brazilians were the ones who built what was later renamed the *Sweetwater* when an American crew claimed salvage rights," Mike Stewart said. "Not knowing what they were getting."

Sue wiped at a glob of brie at the corner of her mouth. "Just their clothes?"

"That's what they do when they feed unchecked," Sonia said. "The other thing they do, is grow. The best feeders eat the runts until there's just a few giants left. That's what the crew of the supply ship found, a handful of big ones hiding deep in the hold. They don't seem crazy about light. Doesn't harm them, but they prefer the dark, like where they hid all those many centuries. Then a rescue team was called in to find the supply crew. Then..."

The Major scooped up the rest of the brie on a wheat cracker. "That's when they called me," he said. "To assess the events here on the rig."

"Rescue the rescue team?" Sue asked.

The Major shook his head. "The Consortium had wised up by then, knew, whatever it was, containment was the only option. Sent in robots with cameras first. Lost three men. We finally sucked the big boys up in some kind of super vacuum the whiz kids at the Consortium cooked up for us."

"All these little ones," Sue asked. "Where did they come from? Can you break them back down into tiny, harmless parts?"

"No," Sonia said, then said no more. It was clear to Sue she was about to hear the really bad news.

Minor apparently picked up on the same bad vibrations. "How fucked are we, Doc?"

It was the Major that cleared his throat. "The pipeline is still intact," he said.

"And," the slender scientist added, "there's more of them down there, lots more, we think."

Minor popped a grape in his mouth. "Then let's cap it and get the fuck outta Dodge."

Sonia shook her head. "The whole thing is unstable," she said. "Along with the crude and a concentration of these things, is a large deposit of natural gas pushing both the oil and the infested slime up the pipeline. From what I know of the projections, the fifteen hundred meters of pipe sitting in the Gulf down there will lose containment within three weeks."

"But," Stewart said, "that timeline, most likely, includes the crew that worked round the clock to maintain the integrity of the pipe."

He marched back to the panel in the bulkhead and hit some buttons on the keyboard. A color-coded bar chart appeared on the monitor. "Good news is, we're still in the green. Pressure is holding solid, for now." He punched a few buttons and the red bar lowered.

"That looks promising," Sue said. "Green is good."

Stewart shook his head. "This is not my department, but I was just scrolling back through readings over the last 72 hours and the pressure is on the rise, more red all the time. Looks like we've got about a day and half before the pipeline blows."

"And all those things are set loose in the Gulf," Sue said. "I don't suppose seawater kills them?"

Sonia shook her head. "They like it just fine."

Stewart put a large paw on her slim shoulder. "But tell them about your findings, Sonia. I don't know much about what these gals are up to, but, from what I've observed, Sonia's the only one to have made hay."

Sonia dragged herself down glumly from a cafeteria tabletop where she had been perching, cross-legged like a middle school girl at an after school club. She looked at Stewart and indicated the bulkhead computer station. "Could you?" Stewart consumed a cracker piled high with slices of cheese, clapped the crumbs from his hands, and slid to the monitor. Sonia pointed at the screen. "Well," she said. "I wasn't getting anywhere for a long time. I had been working with magnetic resonance, using magnetic radiation to set up a field that might disrupt tissues in the creatures. Nothing. Could not generate the power necessary to even pinch the things. After about a week of moping around, that's when I wandered onto the original soundings that uncovered the cache of oil at the bottom of the crust under the Gulf."

Stewart found the file and the embedded screen soon filled with a looping sequence of computer generated animation of a rather crude caliber. It was clear that Sonia was not an expert animator, but equally obvious what the figures on the screen represented.

There was the rig, the *Sweetwater*. Below that, a field of blue that must represent The Gulf, and various striations of brown, displaying Earth's crust, maybe even mantle.

"The *Sweetwater* is a kind of rig known as a spar," Sonia said, walking toward the screen and pointing at various components of the image. "It is a conventional spar with TLP tethers surrounding a single, cylindrical hull..."

"Lady, uh, Sonia," the Major said. "We better get down to the nitty gritty."

The slender woman popped some pretty thick eyeglasses on her narrow nose and pushed a few buttons of her own on the workstation. "What we're about to see is the animation I created based on the numbers recovered from seven soundings, seismic detonations on the floor of the ocean, that are very much like bat sonar. The sound of explosions..."

Impatient, the Major rolled his eyes.

She swallowed hard, continuing. "As you see here: The ripple through the rock should be uniform except where there is something other than rock present. You can see here the crude deposit is shown and a shadow below it. That is the pocket that we believe the entity had been stored in, maybe even thrived. But that's not what is interesting..."

"Nothing about this is interesting," the Major said.

Minor flung a hand toward the now nervous scientist. "Go on, darlin'. You're doing great."

She nodded and went back to the screen. "What's interesting is how, as the shockwave passes through the shadow, the nest of creatures, an answer wave rumbles back up through the crude. It answers, but with more force than the original pulse. And I think I know what it is; it's a rather severe reaction to the amplitude of the wave."

Sonia spun to her audience, clearly excited.

"Don't you see?" she asked. "That kind of reaction? A harsh sound for a harsh sound? To put it simply, if not dramatically, when the shock wave hit the nesting creatures, they screamed."

***

Yes, Sonia, graduate of MIT, had the equipment to end these things, but, as the Major quickly clarified, having the materials is not a plan.

"These things are lethal and proving rather difficult to kill," he said.

"How did you keep them contained at the BioFlouretics plant?" Sue asked him.

The Major flung his hands in the air, flags to his helplessness. "In truth, we didn't," he said. "Any time Doc Oldbridge, or any of her predecessors got one of those things to play with, we had to hold our breath. The more these brainy types poked and prodded at one of these things, the more of my men died." He eyed Sonia. "No offense."

She shook her head. "None taken. I never did have the confidence that these things were contained. But if you can get me to my lab, we can end this."

The Cuban Sue thought as Scarface tossed aside his toothpick. "How come you didn't end this already then, huh?"

"Sonia's work was never taken seriously," Mike Stewart said.

"Sonics?" the Major asked. "Sound?"

Sonia nodded. "I've isolated the sympathetic vibration that will do it. Strangely, these things are rather uniform in their composition, like animate slivers of coal. A single frequency, as sufficiently amplitude would cause rapid liquefaction."

"You mean dissolve?"

"More like explode."

The Major nodded to Stewart. "Show us where her lab is and how to get there."

They gathered around the smallish screen, peering at a tangle of blue lines arranged in sharp-edged geometric figures. Sue was grateful when, after continuing to work the keyboard, Stewart was able to flip the image from a layered top-down perspective to a side view. She recognized the image as a layout of the *Sweetwater*.

"We're here." Stewart stretched as high as he could to indicate a tiny set of paired boxes that was their hiding place, the secondary mess. "Here's Sonia's lab."

"Two decks below," the Major said.

"Yep," Stewart replied.

"And what about the things?" Darren Minor asked. "They...breed...replicate...whatever really quickly. There could be thousands out there, right?"

The question had been directed at the thin scientist who did not respond, only popped off her glasses and rubbed at her sharp chin.

She turned to Stewart. "Cameras are posted in every room of the rig," she said. "The Consortium put in their own after we took over the drill facility. Each is equipped to filter in the infrared band. Also, graphite absorption spectrometers. Mike, could you?"

As Stewart punched up Sonia's request, Sue felt a little left behind. Things were starting to spin out of her wheel house. "The graphite, whatever...what's that going to show?"

Sonia bit her bottom lip and gazed at the screen. "Because the creatures came up through the crude gusher they likely were exposed to radionuclides."

Sue raised a hand and opened her mouth, but Sonia jumped in with a clarification. "All crude oil has trace levels of radioactivity."

"They're radioactive too?" Darren Minor blurted.

The scientist shrugged. "Everything that has spent significant time in the ground has a unique spectral trace. It's from natural decay and release of daughter isotopes from ancient cosmic events. It's not dangerous, but it is unique."

Stewart punched in the last command with a flare. "Got it!"

On the screen, superimposed on the floor plan, were hundreds (thousands, Sue corrected in her mind), of tiny green blips multilayered in many spots, including right outside the hatch to the secondary mess.

Sue was not surprised when some of the men chortled at her response. When she moved firmly into the grandma years, she realized others had certain assumptions about her and what her habits should be. She foiled those expectations now to unintended comic effect.

"Fuck."

They laughed again.

"But it's more than that, a lot more," Darren Minor said to the group. "Am I right?"

The Major nodded. "We're going to need a plan, a multi-layered plan on a tight timeline."

Sonia tapped on the screen where the green blips gathered. "The pressure will blow in the pipeline and then those things will be loose in The Gulf. Once there they can feed on fish, marine mammals, reproduce exponentially. My guess, they'll make it to land within a week. And forget beaches, these things will get into the water system of all the cities on the Gulf, and then…"

There was no need to conclude the statement.

A quiet scratching at the hatch answered. But, they already knew. It was nothing human.

ELEVEN

As far as Sue was concerned, none of the versions of the plan were good. But, they had to do something.

The creatures were all over, not just on the rig, but in the pipe, and, very likely, still in the ground.

But, before all that, Sue, like most in their party, needed a clearer sense of how Sonia's equipment worked and how the little scientist hoped her gadgets would succeed where others had failed.

"Why not just rig up a big version of those guns you gave our giant paramilitary friend here?" Sue asked, jerking a thumb in the Major's direction.

"To my knowledge," Sonia said, scratching at the shoulder straps of a tanktop-over-bra combo, exposing a butterfly tattoo, "the concentrations of the hydrofluoric acid used in the pea-sized ordinance for those guns would be more dangerous than the creatures if put into more widespread use. And the radiation baths used as measures of last resort also would do more harm than good. What I created is an amplified and concentrated focus of hypersonic and subsonic waves that have no danger of spreading. They're very focused, like a sound laser."

Darren Minor reached for the acoustic he had scrounged from some crewman's quarters before having to hole-up in the auxiliary mess. "Amplification," he said, strumming a chord, "that's my specialty."

"Actually," Sonia said, her eyes glazing to her thinking place, "there may be a way to offer a demonstration without my equipment. It won't be as effective, but the principle would be the same. Can that guitar be hooked up like an electric guitar."

Minor turned over the Fender. "It has a jack so it can hook up to an amplifier."

"Or a PA system?"

Minor shrugged, "Sure."

Sonia turned to Stewart, who put up a stop sign hand. "I'm on it."

"Wait!" the bandana sporting roadie shouted. "It seems to me, every time you white lab coat types play with these things, the situation goes all Manson Family at Roman Polanski's house, know what I mean, man?"

Sonia seemed locked onto what Mike was up to, speaking without looking at the man. "This will be safe. The signal will be projected throughout the rig while we remain secure in here. Stuffing our ears with something might be in order."

"Well," bandana man said, "if you're looking to make guitar noise that makes ears bleed, I'm your man."

"We're good," Stewart interjected, also without looking at the roadie.

"Hey! Were you there in '75 when this man was playing in a driving rain at the Charlotte Speedway when half the band got electrocuted, were you--"

Minor put a gentle, spider-fingered hand on his tour-mate's shoulder. "Let 'em be," he said. "They'll find out, sooner or later, in a pinch, you're the best noise engineer this side of marmalade skies."

The scientist glanced away from the monitor in the wall, looking for something. "Now to hook up the guitar."

Sue saw Minor and his roadie exchange glances. "See, Shroom?" Minor said with a wry smile.

The roadie named Shroom (no need to guess why), flipped from back-to-front a fanny pack Sue had missed. *Am I getting old?* She wondered, finding her generally optimistic and adventurous demeanor had taken some dings. She felt old, end of the road old. *But, I can't afford to feel that way.*

Shroom, satisfied smile on his unshaven face, handed a little box with an antenna to Stewart and handed a similar black box with a guitar jack protruding from one end to his boss. Minor reached under the curvaceous bottom end of the Fender and plugged the box into the guitar. Stewart eyed his box, also with a jack, and found the appropriate spot on the wall panel to plug it in.

Shroom eyed Sue. "Wireless unit," he said and winked.

"Play," Stewart said over his shoulder to Minor.

Part of Sue still harbored some awe for the owner of her new home and winner of a belated Grammy for his underwhelming album from the '80's called *And a Bottle of Rum*.

The acoustic fed a silent signal into the wireless, but also poured forth into the all metal room a kind of warmth that fed parts of Sue the brie cheese could not.

Sue quickly recognized the chord progression of *Bar Mangled Manners*, and she remembered friends, cute sandals she had just bought at Mandies and a flower some random boy had placed in her hair, the warmth of the red wine lining her innards.

The memory was quickly interrupted. "Not songs!" Sonia yelled at the yacht rock god.

Obviously not a fan.

"Not songs," she said again, a bit milder, "noises. Somewhere on that fretboard has to be the frequency we need, once you hit it, I'll know and can modulate it and amplify it. Then I will broadcast it throughout the ship. It won't kill them all, but I can show you how it works."

"May even clear a path," Scar the Cuban said.

"Doubtful," Sonia said. She turned to Minor. "We need something with a frequency in the twenty hertz range."

Minor eyed Shroom who smiled knowingly. "E flat, moving toward E," he said.

Minor's spidery fingers found the spot.

The tiny speakers in the wall unit crackled and then offered a scratchy version of the rich chord the master's fingers released from the receptive Fender.

Sonia watched a yellow waveform on the screen appear on the monitor where a green line already curled. They were a bit out of sync.

"Almost," Sonia said. "A bit higher."

Still powerful, the wrinkled fingers pulled down on the strings, bending the notes upward.

"Higher."

Sue didn't know much about guitars, but she knew this: acoustic strings were not meant to be bent. But special muscles trained by half a century of playing bent the strings higher.

Sonia tapped the screen. "Okay," Sonia said, "we have the frequency but we're not getting the amplitude necessary from your side to make it of any use."

"Already dialed the thing up to ten," Minor said.

Then dial it up to eleven. Where had Sue heard the ridiculous assertion?

Shroom sighed and grabbed his boss by the elbow. Minor hung tight to the chord, letting himself be led from his spot on the table top where he could let the guitar ride his knee like a schoolgirl. As they got closer to the wall speakers, a feedback loop grew until an ear dagger sliced the room.

Sonia uncovered her ears, grabbed for a napkin, tore off a piece and wadded the bits in her ears. The tilt of her head indicated everyone should do the same. Shroom and Minor begged off.

"Won't be necessary darlin."

"Then let it loose, Mike," Sonia yelled so Stewart could hear through the soft paper in his ears.

Ears aren't the only organ sensitive to sound, Sue realized as a pulse shivered through her and her teeth started to ache like a mad dentist giving her dental work a good poke.

The glass top to a cruet of salad dressing exploded. The remainder of the brie bubbled and burned.

To let loose the pain from the rape of her teeth, Sue released a sound that might ordinarily be a scream but could not be perceived except for an ache in her throat.

A tear ran down her cheek. Sue put hands on either side of her head to stop it from becoming brie cheese.

Then it stopped.

Minor and Shroom turned to one another. "How're your ears?"

"Huh?" Minor said, then smiled. "A little buzzy. Reminds me of rehearsals in small studios with large amps."

Sue wrenched her jaw back and forth as though she was in an airplane that had just reached maximum altitude.

Sonia walked toward the hatch.

"Wait!" the Cuban with the scar yelled. "What are you doing?"

"Seeing what we got." She opened the door where death had been scratching a short time ago.

"No!" tThey yelled together.

But scientists have to know what damage their toys wreak.

Sue felt some relief when the woman slipped lengthy gloves from a side pocket in her cargo pants and slipped them on with a rubbery squeak. That relief evaporated when Sonia hunched down, and just out of sight, appeared to reach for something on the floor, the only place the creatures could be without infiltrating a standing host.

Sure enough, Sonia stood holding it like a sliver of steak over an invisible dog. The latching mechanism for the hatch obscured the rest of the hallway.

"See?" she said. "Dead. And if you could see, there are a few dozen more out here like it or in worse shape."

Sonia stepped over the lip of the hatchway, with the supposedly dead creature between pursed fingers. The entire company recoiled, but responded with absolute shock when Sonia stepped fully into the room and there was another creature, unseen by the slender scientist, on the back of her cargo pants.

Mike Stewart reached out from across the room as though to grab for the thing with his desperation. "Sonia!"

She looked down, and, upon seeing her stowaway, began swatting at it.

The Major leapt forward. "No!" he growled. "Stop, you'll set if free in here. It must be stunned or it would be loose and on the attack. Get me something to put it in from the kitchen."

A plastic pitcher was produced. The Major looked doubtfully at the container but accepted it from Shroom. He turned to Sonia. "Give me one of your gloves."

The Major jammed the lengthy glove on his right arm and then shakily removed the stunned super leech from Sonia's pants, disheartened to see a hole where the thing's mouth had locked on. It left behind a ring of blood on Sonia's leg.

"Hey," Sonia said, seeming to see the Major for the first time. "You're black!"

The Major capped the beverage pitcher. "Put this in the freezer and then tape the freezer shut."

Sonia spotted Darren Minor. "You're...you're..."

Minor swelled a bit with modesty. "Well, yes, but..."

"You're Steve Miller, aren't you?"

Shroom laughed. Minor sucked at his teeth and tucked the guitar away beneath a table.

"My mother turned me onto your stuff, man," Sonia continued, her eyes a bit glazed. "*Jungle Love*, dig that tune, man."

"Get her up on a table," the Major ordered.

Sonia looked distractedly dismayed as she was hoisted by the Major and Scarface up onto a table and encouraged to lay prone. "Hey! I'm not a puppet! You can't pull my strings."

"Quiet Kermit," the Major said. He dug a gloved finger into the hole the stunned creature had made and ripped it open. "Get me a knife!"

"What are you going to do?" Sue asked.

Sonia struggled on the table. "I'm going to give you one chance to read me a bedtime story, Grandma. Just one chance!"

The Major ignored what Sonia said but pointed at the wild look in her eyes. "Clearly there's a toxin. What would you do if it had been a snake?"

Sue held out a weak, age spotted, cautionary hand. "Oh...I don't think..."

Sue's objection was a deer running in front of a freight train. The Major took the paring knife a nameless 'Cuban' handed him. "Hold her."

"Hold me tight. Like you mean it, baby."

The Major cleared off the light smear of blood with his gloved hand, revealing a single, shallow mark that looked like a cigarette burn. He made a longitudinal slice across the mark, blood flowing freely. The Major leaned down toward the wound he had made.

Sue's warning hand gained strength. "Wait!" she yelped. "At least, before you engage in that bit of disgusting madness, tell me your real name."

The Major laughed, leaned down and put his mouth to the flowing blood. His lips moved with vampiric delight over the wound. He sat up and spat then returned to the wound. He did this three times. After the third drawing out of the hallucinogenic toxin, a little less vehement than the first, he stood up, wavering a bit on his feet.

Scarface held up a hand to steady him.

"I'm fine."

Sonia let a short-nailed finger trace a pocket in the Major's militaristic cargo pants. "You sure are fine."

"Shroom," Minor said. "Looks like those things out there are a little worse-for-wear or they'd be in here drilling for oil in each of us. *BUT* I know we'd all feel better if you'd saunter over there and shut that hatch."

The look that briefly washed across Shroom's stubbled, florid face said *Who me?* But he went. And Sue did feel better when the three inch steel hatch once again separated her from the dangers of the rest of the rig.

"Okay," Darren Minor said. "Her mojo works. She dealt those things a pretty good blow."

Sonia slipped from the table to her feet, swinging her arms up into the stiff rictus of air guitar. "Mr. Mojo Rising!"

Mike Stewart put a calming paw on one of the slender shoulders. "Not even with her equipment," he said. "You should see what her stuff can do when she gets it hooked up."

"Yeah, bitch! See what I can do!"

Sue felt her nose crinkle without her permission, then when she caught the smile on Shroom's face, she let out the laugh. "I'm sorry." Sue pulled herself together, remembering she was likely to die here on this failed oil rig in the middle of the flooded meteor crater known as The Gulf of Mexico. "The...the question is; how do we get to her equipment? Clearly, even stunned, those things are way too dangerous to walk through."

The Major crossed the room, put his large hands on either of Sue's shoulders and looked her meaningfully in the eyes. Sue dropped her eyes. She didn't really need a pep talk. The Major lifted her by the chin so that they locked eyes, his full of intent. "Wilber," he said. "My name is Wilber."

TWELVE

"Yes," Stewart said, "I can rig it up again. Sure, another blast, but you saw what you got. It's like walloping them in the head."

"May have killed a few," Darren Minor said, already hoisting the acoustic and turning on his end of the wireless unit. "Could get lucky and kill a few more."

The Major sat between them on a table bench, closely trimmed head in ebony hands. He did not look up.

"We could," Stewart said. He didn't seem all that enthusiastic about starting the procedure up again. Part of Sue was grateful. She wondered what it was like to have your teeth explode in your mouth. "Then tip-toe through the remainders and hope they're not frisky enough to run us through like lamb on a spit."

"We don't have a choice," Sue said. "Time is running out. If the pipe blows then I'm betting we'll be battling those things on a sinking rig."

"We have no time," a deep voice said from the middle of the room. The Major lifted his head. "When we arrived, there were a series of storms brewing up from the south east. If the pipeline doesn't blow by then, spreading those things for miles, it will when a tropical storm comes rolling in."

"So," Minor said, "we'll let 'er rip, suit up as best we can and get Sonia down to her lab."

"Let errrrr rip!" Sonia blurted from where she stretched prone on a cafeteria table, semiconscious.

"It's not much of a plan," Stewart said.

The Major stood, rubbing his temples. "It all works if we get Sonia to her lab, even just one of us. We have more than one threat to deal with. Meanwhile, Mike, can we raise the Coast Guard on that thing?"

Stewart tossed up his hands. "It's against protocol. We're not even supposed to exist."

"Neither should those things," Sue said.

"We're going to need some backup here," the Major said. "You stay here. If you don't get a signal from us, send out a message to whoever will listen, include all the data on the creatures."

Stewart did not look happy about any of those tasks. "If you say so."

The Cubans came out of the kitchen, fistsful of black plastic garbage bags held out before them. "These may buy us a few seconds, important seconds, to keep moving. Sometimes, it's just about going forward."

"Amen brother," the Major said.

"I think I have those lyrics in a song," the king of yacht rock said, checking the tuning on the guitar.

The second time was worse.

Sue still had some of her own teeth mixed in with bridgework, dentures on top. When it was done, Sue could feel the bits of crumbled bridgework floating around in her mouth. Now she'd need dentures on top and bottom.

As a child, taking swim lessons at the YMCA, Sue had accepted a dare to swim to the bottom of the deep end of the pool. This sonic attack was like that first adventure to the deep end. An enormous pressure sought to crush her skull like a pair of giant pliers about to crack a walnut.

When she heard one of the big men cry out, Sue felt a little proud--never mind she was afraid to open her mouth for fear that her various forms of false teeth would melt out. Then the pain focused into a pinpoint of white pain right between her eyes. She thought she smelled burning hair.

Then it ended. Sue thought she would not be able to recover. She ran her tongue over her mouth. She felt better and her teeth did not melt.

The next step was to find a way to offer the team some minimal protection.

Three layers of garbage bags secured by rubber bands around her legs did not do much to add a sense of security for Sue. The men offered to let her stay with Mike. But, as the Major had said, if just one of them gets Sonia to her lab, it could make all the difference. It did not matter who got her there, even a grandmother to five, wonderful grandkids.

All but Mike ventured out into the hallway. The Major was able to establish radio contact with Stewart.

The creatures in the passageway did not move. Some had essentially fallen apart. There were a few large ones among them where the process of cannibalism, a sort of concentration of the things, had started.

The make-shift platoon featured Minor at the point (two tours in Vietnam) with Shroom right behind him. The last of the BioFlouretic agents were third in line. They put Sue in the middle, the least vulnerable position. The two Cubans were next with the Major taking up the rear.

The BioFlouretic agent, one of the many men who hid behind hazmat suits for so long, had one of the acid guns, a few acid pellets left, so Sue was told.

That agent could not resist kicking one of the immobile, black squiggles. Sue tensed, almost yelping, but it did not retaliate.

The multi-layered garbage bags rasped brittlely as Sue tip-toed through the slurry of half-pulped super leeches.

We're never going to make it. She wanted to scream it, would make her feel better to scream, but she held it inside.

A hand came up to cover Sue's eyes but it was too late. There were bodies, horrible forms torn so completely and cleanly that even a glance offered a clear vantage on exposed bone through runnels of meat.

Whoever thought to cover her eyes, Sue was grateful. They even guided her along. Then the first commotion erupted.

The hands came off. Bodies were everywhere, but little blood. Someone up front was dancing about and others in the line were responding. It was difficult to tell from Sue's vantage--and she was sore pressed to get closer-- but it appeared Darren Minor happened upon one of the larger ones, stepping on it where it had been hiding beneath a layer of melted small ones, eating their remains. It was sluggish, but plenty awake and gripping the aging rock star.

Minor pranced and slapped at the creature, holding a loose garbage bag in his hands. No daq-head, the thing used slippery fins to cling tenuously to the makeshift wading boots of garbage bags. While the others slapped at the thing, Minor wore out his upper range, screeching.

They slapped at it, too afraid to make substantial contact with the two foot-long distillation of midnight. Once knocked to the floor, Minor danced back, opening a space between himself and the flopping, seeking eel. The BioFlouretic agent stepped forward and used up a round of acid. He missed.

Sue counted with each breath the next three misses. He killed it on the fifth shot, melting its head (the general region of the hunting mouth). Sue did not know how many more sticky acid bullets remained. She knew they had a way to go. Schematics showed they had to cross this deck and climb down to the lower decks, traversing the length of level three to the lab.

During the danger, the Major hoisted Sonia over one massive shoulder.

Minor took a shaky breath. They looked at the acid gun. The agent checked the chamber and shook his head.

"One left," he said.

"Will have to make it a good one," Scarface said.

"Let's go," the Major said, returning Sonia to her feet. She wobbled and held her head in hands but looked cogent. "We have to push forward."

They stepped over the bodies and made their way to the passage opening onto access points to the decks below.

The plan, as stated, was to climb down the maintenance ladder to level three. Sue was not sure her shaky legs would hold her while trying to maintain a grip on the metal tube rungs. There was an elevator.

Sue put a shaky hand to her rubbery legs. "Maybe we could revisit taking the elevator. Not sure I'm up to the climb."

"We went over this, Sue," the Major said. "We have those storms coming in, and we don't want to get caught in there if a precocious flash of lightning finds its way to the rig."

"Could be the elevator is floor-to-ceiling with these things," Shroom threw in.

The area immediately surrounding their transit options looked clear to Sue, so she walked around the trees of men that had bunched up in the alcove. Sue peered down the tube that hosted the gamut of steel rail rungs. After the first four rungs, the ladder option looked like five miles of pitch black.

It was barely a step to reach across and push the elevator call button, and she did. It responded with a celebratory ding. The men, caught up in a quick review of the next actions steps, turned to Sue and the elevator in horror.

Darren Minor, who still looked a bit shook up from his battle with the alien death eel, openly cringed. "Uh, Sue…"

The doors rolled open smoothly, quietly; emblematic of the care put into the rig during the science Consortium's retrofit of the oil sucker into a high tech eel stopper. All eyes went to the floor of the elevator compartment. The floor was bare.

Sue turned and offered the big strong men a look saying, *You Scaredy Cats!*

She proceeded to step into the compartment.

"Sue! No!"

Several pair of strong hands grabbed old shoulders that hadn't done anything more strenuous for the last few years than croquet on the Minor Mansion's lawn.

"Oww!" Sue yelped, not seriously hurt, but surprised.

The Major spun her on her heels and looked her directly in the eyes. "Sue!" he grumbled. "You need to follow my lead, Ms. Mayfield. Our best chance of keeping our group whole is stick to the plan. Do you follow me?"

Sue nodded, hurt but also sure that this was treatment not offered to any of the men in the group. The Major, like the rest of them, looked stricken. Their favorite grandma had almost gotten eaten by slugs from hell right before their horrified eyes.

Darren Minor pushed his way through the thicket of nervous men. "Sue," he said, tenderly, "that thing is a cannister of death. There are so many gaps and spaces those things could have slipped into."

"And we'd be trapped in there with them," Shroom offered.

The Major, having calmed some, left his hand on Sue's shoulder but kept it gentle. "Stick to *the plan*, Sue. Okay?"

Sue bit her bottom lip before answering. "I just know...that ladder looks awfully long and dark."

The Major straightened and looked up at the ceiling in exasperation. He appeared to regret having brought the old woman along.

"Do you think you could hold onto my shoulders while we climb down?" he asked.

Sue did not feel any better about this proposal, perhaps worse.

"I don't know," she said. "Maybe I should go back."

Scarface stepped forward. "Ma'am, we're way past that now. We must go forward."

Sue glanced at the gaping hole with the first rung just visible.

"Oh," she said, "no, I'll be okay. I'll be better off changing hands than trying to hold tight. But I'm afraid that I might get winded and have to stop."

"You'll go second to last," the Major said. "I'll be with you in the rear. I won't let you get hurt."

Sue looked at the pit they were about to willingly climb into and felt her heart offer a single throb of protest.

The men had flashlights that they managed to strap to various parts of their bodies to throw shuffling light over their passage. Sonia had regained herself and was making good time up front with Scarface and Darren Minor.

Sue tried not to look down. She was not afraid of heights, but to look down with the swirling bars of light from the loosely bound flashlights might cause her to vomit. Worse than that would be to look down and be denied sight of the bottom. Sue's rational mind assured her the platoon was no more than five minutes into the dark artery. A more persuasive voice called from the skittish animal inside her. They were never going to reach the end of this ladder.

She looked forward, taking some time to remind herself that she was not alone in the swirling darkness; Sue looked up. That's when she noted that the tunnel had a cap.

A circle of steel, painted black, stopped up the top of the maintenance tube like a cork.

Sue pointed this out, hoping hearing it out loud would further ease her mind. "Looks like we won't get caught in the rain," she said, pointing at the black cover that she just noted had a fine sheen to it. "That looks pretty solid."

The Major peered upward in the dazzle of battling beams. "Yeah." He really did not give it a look, carefully shuffling a booted foot to a lower rung while positioning himself to make a grab for Sue if she should falter. But then he stopped.

The Major looked up into the dark where the pitch stopper protected them from above. Then he grabbed for his own flashlight and unhooked it from a utility loop in his navy seal cargo pants. He angled the flashlight. Sue stopped at the Major's sudden attention to what Sue took as a point of security. He moved deliberately, running the circle of light over their head cover with the focus of a veteran of trouble, deep trouble.

"What?" Sue asked, now nervous about the black stopper. "What is it?"

The Major did not respond for a moment, squinting up into the gloom. "I...uh, nothing, Sue, noth..."

It moved. Or Sue thought it did. Her glasses were new. They were good, but she was not as sharp-eyed as her twenty-four-year-old self.

The Major, to Sue's frustration, dropped the flashlight beam. She was about to cry out, but she could see what he was doing. He wiped at a sheen of sweat at his brow, took a labored breath and raised the light again. He wanted to be sure.

Sue could hear the voices of the others from what seemed far below them, bouncing up the yards of surrounding steel.

She gaped up at the plug in the tube, that just moments ago seemed to be their backup, anchoring the climb, getting their back. She had thought it a feature of the rig, some sort of hatch. Now she held her breath, waiting to confirm some new nightmare.

It had a texture; she could see it. Little rivulets and bumps like the skin on a teenager's backside. She looked and looked, and before it moved again, to confirm the worst, she saw that it had dimension; it bulged in their direction.

Then it did move.

"Go, Sue!"

She did not have to be told.

She knew she would fall, but did not care.

There was a sickly, wet sound as the giant eel from space uncoiled itself, or rather, squirmed to free its girth from where it had wedged itself in its search for more meat, human or its fellow super slugs, whatever it could grow huge on.

Sue fumbled down the steel rungs, sure she would slip and get one in the back of the head as she tumbled.

The Major made no attempt to follow.

"Come on!" Sue called after him.

He did not respond, his face set in obsidian cool. He reached down and grabbed Sue roughly by the wrist. Before she could yelp, he lifted her from her position on the ladder, crazily drawing her up toward the monster above. Then he held her still, having plucked her from the ladder like pulling a cat from its comfy place, claws out. He winked.

Then dropped her.

Her heart leapt from her chest. When she cried out, it was not out of fear for herself but for the Major, who receded as she fell into the black, some of that black a giant eater of all things living, falling on her protector and ripping him to shreds. The moments it took to devour him, would buy the rest of them time.

She landed on someone, someone with a very real complaint.

News of the attack spread through the rest of group. Sue was enveloped in big man arms and transported down the rungs as many at a time as terrified hands could grasp. The last of the BioFlouretic agents cried out to his commander but was thwarted by his position in the pack and forced down the rungs.

To her regret, Sue was cradled in a position where she had a good vantage up the tube.

If someone had suggested to her that the Major was the one person who would not scream when being devoured by a giant leech, Sue would buy the premise. But he screamed.

In the flailing arch of his flashlight, Sue could see the short-lived battle. Caught in a feeding frenzy, the thing thrashed and coiled about the Major as he struck uselessly at the thing's impenetrable black flesh. A drop of blood landed on Sue's cheek. She yelped.

The Major swelled as the unnamed creature dug its way into his torso. Like a goliath hand forcing its way into an ill-fitting glove, the creature swelled through the man Sue could never think of as Wilber.

The group was down, boots on the ground, or on a covering of small super slugs and their remains after the second wave of the guitar bomb. Sue was jostled as the men danced out of the sluggish creatures to a bare spot in the lower hallway. As they reached the fringe of the puddle of alien maggots, they could clearly hear the giant coming down the tube.

Scarface shoved at the reticent BioFlouretic agent. "Come on!"

Sue told herself not to look behind her. Look what happened to Lot's wife, she told herself. But it was one of those cases of the rebelling brain. Don't think of pink elephants, and that's the image conjuring itself into your noggin.

A leg dropped out of the access tube into the pile of sleepy creatures with a splat. The baby eels played at the stump. A moment later, the giant fell on the leg and the little monsters.

That's when the little ones came to life. Suspecting they were about to end up in the gullet of their big brother, the babies squiggled and flopped away from the giant cannibal covering them.

The team slipped down the congested hallway, most of them taking frightened glances back at the scene unfolding behind them. Even more frightened than the humans were the little creatures that fought and flailed as they were sucked up like black pasta into the giant's hungry mouth.

"That won't last long," Darren Minor said. He turned toward Sonia. "Which way?"

Sonia pointed, fully alert now. "This way," she said. "Straight ahead."

They moved ahead at a quick shuffle Sue doubted she could maintain. Quickly winded, Sue glanced behind her.

It did not last long. The biggie was flopping down the compartment, humping and thumping along like a mega inchworm.

Three yard worm, Sue thought and tried to push her tired feet along.

A few stray little ones littered the passageway. Sue was sweating profusely. The others were too. Little drops of what had to be sweat dribbled onto one of Sue's bare arms.

A drop here and then another.

Damn, these guys are sweaty.

When she looked down, the drops were black and oblong.

No. They were tiny monster slugs.

Sue screamed and started smacking at herself. She stopped and looked up and another tiny black worm landed on her forehead, having dropped from an overhead ventilator.

Then they were all dancing and smacking at themselves. And removing clothing.

Small as mealworms, the things were flicked away easy enough, dripping out of their hiding place, dazed. The mission had been halted though; not one of them wanted to chance having a worm hiding somewhere in a collar or a waistband.

The giant, not nearly as stunned as the little ones, thumped down the passageway after them.

"We gotta move!" Shroom yelled, whipping off his bandana and shaking loose whatever nasties may have slipped into its folds.

"They're all over!" Sue cried, abandoning a sensible swatting of worms and began clawing at her face.

A hand reached out and stopped her. It was Darren Minor. He hunched and looked her in the face. He did not have a shirt on. "Sue, swat, not scratch. And do your swatting as we move. This way, Sue, straight ahead."

He pulled her forward and sacrificed his own personal debugging to look Sue over and pick at the few remaining malignant maggots from her shirt and hair. "How will I know?" Sue asked.

He pulled her forward and peeking into his shorts. "Know what, Sue?"

"That anything is real from this point on?" she asked. "How many of the little ones bit me, even just nibbled?"

"Well," Minor said, apparently satisfied with his inspection of his undies, "stick with me, Suzie-Q cause if anyone has built up an immunity to hallucinogens, it would be Shroom and I. We'll keep you on the straight and narrow."

He gave her a wink.

They moved, but something in Sue cried out a warning. Her skin crawled, certain hundreds of the deadly little wigglers were busying themselves digging into her skin, already paper thin with age.

They moved forward.

"Just this way," Sonia said.

Sue's arms were bare. She had lost the light sweater, the one with the roses, somewhere in the journey. No worms popped out of her skin. This allowed her feet to shuffle on.

Sue scanned her shirtless companions, watching for little black heads popping out of their backs, for a worm not quite as sleepy as they all hoped. Then the mayhem would return, alien leeches slipping in and out of human flesh as easily as dolphins breaching water. And they would instantly multiply in their blood bath, plenty of baby eels for all of them.

Sue's pulse raced until she felt heady. She spoke to distract herself. "What are they called?"

The group glanced at her, including Sonia, who the question had been aimed at. She looked directly at Sonia and asked again. "Haven't you named these things yet? They're a new discovery. I'd have assumed you scientists would be falling all over each other to claim the discovery and put your brand on them."

Sonia thought this over, allowing herself to be urged on by the men. "The Consortium has all intellectual rights, but I'm guessing they'd be open to suggestions. Often scientific names are based on physical attributes and who knows those better than those here on the rig?"

"Name it after me?" Sue asked.

Sonia looked puzzled for a moment as though Sue played a joke, but then the narrow woman smiled. "Sure, Sue. Why not?"

"My maiden name is Platt," Sue said.

Sonia considered for a moment. "The Latin name for flatworm phylum is *platyhelminthes*. And...uh, the latin class name for black-eyed Susans is hirta. So, uh…"

Verbal creativity not her strong suit, the wordsmith that once wrote the lyrics *If it ain't fixed, not your business to straighten it. The sea blew a breeze long before you stretched out a blanket...* cleared his throat to offer a title. Heck, he had a song on the top 100 am radio playlist he entitled *Hibiscus On My Shirt*.

"*Hirt Plattus*," Minor offered.

Sonia cleared her throat. They were inches away from the hatch to the lab. "Well, uh, think you got the order mixed up, uh...phylum and class...never mind. *Hirt Plattus,* perfect!"

The lab required handprint entry. Sonia slapped her palm on the gently glowing screen stationed by the double receding hatchway.

The doors separated with a pneumatic hiss. The group shuffled into the doorway.

Inside the lab, among a scatter of broken glass and displaced monitors, four giant mega eels hunted, slapping what Sue took as tails between tabletops still hosting technical devices alien to Sue but what she instantly trusted as suitable to Sonia's work.

"Get the fuck out of there," the skinny scientist yelped. "That's my work!"

Darren Minor gaped at the four monsters that hadn't yet detected the human presence. "What now?" he asked.

It was the lead of the Cubans, Scarface, that answered.

"What else is there?" he said. "Draw them out, one at a time and kill them."

Shroom and Minor exchanged looks.

Shroom asked the Cuban agent. "How do we make that work?"

"Yes!" Sonia said. "Distract them. Draw them away from the equipment, and I'll do the rest."

The men eyed one another and shrugged, sharing some secret code only those hyperly endowed with excess testosterone would know. The remaining agent who had served under the Major raised his specially constructed weapon and fired a sticky bit of highly concentrated acid to burn off the front end of the nearest super eel. It fell to the deck. The remaining three quickly picked up on the source of the aggression and began flopping in the direction of the entry hatch.

THIRTEEN

Sue was transported, for a moment, to when she was a child and a rabid dog got loose in the family house. Haphazard and demented, it worked its way toward Sue (aged ten) and her younger sister, Steph (aged eight), in convulsive shivers of its limp-legged frame. It never made it near them. Dad owned a shotgun.

The giant mega eels, fully grown *Hirt Plattus*, snaked toward the open hatch with blind precision. Having miscalculated the acid gun ordinance, the BioFlouretic agent shot the next nearest beast, bisecting the anaconda-thick undulating black. But no such luck on the next, dry trigger. Now there truly were no more whining acid bullets.

Sue felt sure, like other primitive, limacine creatures, the splitting of the super disgusting creatures would cause them to grow where they had been cut. Where there had been four, soon there'd be eight.

Sue turned to Sonia. "More acid," she said, "you must have some in here. It's a laboratory."

"It's not that kind of lab," Sonia said. Like the group as a whole, they stood transfixed watching the remaining blind monsters seek them out.

"Toss some chemicals on the things. Maybe they'll catch fire or something," Sue said.

Sonia slapped her hands on her thighs. "It's not that kind of lab! Okay!" she shouted. "It's a sonics lab. See the speakers?"

Then Sue did see the room a little better. Beyond the terror slowly approaching them, the materials in the room, still largely whole, seemed a clutter of instruments. The speakers were the clearest indication of the lab's purpose. There were towers of black boxes and disembodied cones dangling from wires so slim, the unsecured speakers seemed to float about the space like Peter Pan visiting Wendy Darling's room.

"If you could get me in there," Sonia said. "Get me to that wall panel, there. I can kill these things."

The bulkhead that hosted the imbedded workstation seemed five miles away.

"We'll never make it," Shroom said.

Darren Minor sighed and ran a hand through his still lustrous, gray hair. "Sonia," he said, "what do you know about these things? You guys must have been able to pick up something about them, observed something helpful?"

A distant rumble of thunder preceded the urgent howl of a powerful wind against the rusted hull of the oil rig.

"Storm's rolling in," Scarface said.

Minor nodded. "Time is not on our side. We'll lose power if that storm starts spitting lightning our way."

"I'll need power to run my equipment," Sonia said. "What do I know about these things? I know if we don't stop them, here, now, they'll be the only things living in Minor Mansions two days from now."

"That's not really helpful to the situation at hand," Sue said.

Sonia eyed her, but then looked away at the windows that spanned the third of the lab's bulkhead. Her eyes glazed a bit behind the thick-framed glasses.

"They are blind, as far as we could tell," Sonia said. "Experiments could not positively determine how they locate prey. Some thought it was a chemical trace, sniffing out blood. And I'd accept that, however, what also could be true is vibrations."

"As in sounds?" Sue asked.

Sonia nodded. "And of movement in much the same way a spider can tell something is stuck in its web. I was not able to prove this in any substantial way, but my results were no less conclusive than most of what had been accomplished here. Generally, I was left out in the cold, not part of the main group. But, I can tell you they are sensitive to sympathetic vibrations."

Shroom chuckled. "Hah."

Darren Minor wore a similar grin.

"What?" Sue asked.

"These things are Beach Boys fans," Shroom said.

Sonia nodded and paced furiously in the double-wide hatch to her lab, ignoring the creeping death a couple of yards into the room. "Exactly," she said, "harmonies, yes, the Beach Boys. Compared to other researchers, I was rather underfunded. However, see those windows? No other lab has windows like those. They're a special kind of plexiglass composite with an exterior STC of 64."

Shroom nodded. "Nice."

"But on the interior section is double paned with a lead treated polycarbonate that not only bounces back sounds to a particular focal point in the room, but regulates the frequency, it uh…"

"Mellows the high and lows," Shroom said. "This place is one big sound booth."

Sonia nodded. "Essentially," she said, "the focal point is about three meters off the center of the floor. If we could build up a certain amplitude of sound at various points of the outside of the room, the sound will gather and grow there and the entities will draw away from the outside of the lab and concentrate in the middle."

"It will give us some wiggle room," Scarface said.

"If only we had the guitar," Sonia said.

Minor laughed and touched her shoulder. "You forgot already?" he asked. "Beach Boys, Sonia. Harmonies?"

Shroom gave a her shoulder a friendly poke. "We brought the instruments with us. We can all sing."

"Speak for yourself," Sue said. "I'd always mumble the words to hymns in church. I got the voice of an air raid siren."

"Well, siren," Minor said. "Sing your siren song. From what Sonia says, those windows will do most of the work, and I'll do my best to keep everyone on pitch. What's the notes, Sonia."

"Uh, 415.3 hertz is optimal," Sonia said.

Shroom considered for a moment. "A-Flat."

"I'll do my best to find it. I--"

Scarface cleared his throat. "I have perfect pitch. I can hit it."

Minor nodded. "And I'll help build harmonies, a chord, on it."

Sue looked at the stout dark-haired man with the scar. "You're not Cuban, are you?"

He shook his head. "I was born in Belgium."

"Who are you guys?" Sue asked, glancing at Scarface's compatriot.

It was Sonia who responded. "There are forces at work here, players that act when something fantastic happens, something cataclysmic. They're a part of it. I'm a part of it. The Major was a part of it."

"I'm here," Scarface said, "because that's where I'm supposed to be. This is where the players have to be right now to save the world."

Sue nodded, "So, go ahead," she said. "Sing your note and save the world."

They moved gingerly into the room. Down from an even eight to lucky seven, four followed Darren Minor along the bulkhead to the left, this included the centerpiece to the plan, Dr. Sonia Revere, associate professor of applied sciences at CalTech.

Sue was the middle dancer in a three person kickline, the ones she could only think of as Cubans, bookending.

Still somewhat stunned by that last guitar bomb, the blind passage of the giant eel things shifted slightly from the center-cleared of equipment toward the edges where the terrified dance troupe tread.

The two remaining giant masses of squirming blackness huddled roughly in the middle of the room.

The group transformed from dance troupe to expectant choir as they established optimal spread, turning toward the center of the room and the death occupying the middle.

"About there," Sonia said, indicating the center of the room closer to the high ceiling than the top of her head. She held an arm up. "You should all do as I do," she said. "It will help to establish a certain degree of precision."

They all pointed at the spot, sighting down their arms like snipers with high powered rifles.

"Mr. Shroom?" Minor said to the much shorter man next to him.

Shroom dropped his arm long enough to extract a device from his fanny pack. "Give me a sec," he said concentrating on the small box.

"Don't think we got one, Shroomy," Minor said.

Shroom held up a finger asking for another *sec*. Then smiled. He pressed a red button on top of the box and a tone issued into the room. Minor cleared his throat.

"Is that the note?" Sue asked.

Shroom shook his bandana cover head.

"That's A," Scarface said.

"Don't worry; he'll find it," Minor replied.

Darren Minor gave another little cough, and in a suave tenor hit the A. Even Sue could tell there was slight dissonance. Scarface kicked in and straightened out Minor's tone. The note slipped out of Minor like a water glass slowly sliding across the condensation on a stone table.

"That's the one," Shroom said, and clearing his own throat, let slip a quavering note that mostly seemed to blend with the A-flat floating in the room. One-by-one they all joined in. Sue's voice felt worn, her throat ached but she sang the note.

The creatures stopped.

Then the note seemed to grow in the air on its own, warming the air around them, soothing them, encouraging them until the note filled Sue with a warm tingle, like after a couple of healthy belts of chardonnay.

The creatures squirmed away from the edges toward the center.

"Keep it up," Sonia said, slipping from the group, moving without concern among the equipment.

The note did not suffer from her loss; in fact, Minor added a harmony that was topped by Scarface, and the note grew to a heavenly chorus that made Sue feel as though her feet were leaving the ground.

And then she did. She was floating. Part of her always knew Darren Minor would do this for her one day, allow her to transcend, whole-bodied, up to rock-n-roll heaven. But the impression ripened a bit, rotting on the vine. She thought maybe she'd stopped singing. Some part of her thought to stick a finger in the waistband of her soiled white shorts and check there for ticks; they like to burrow in on those tights spots. Another part of her knew she was not looking for ticks and the things in the center of the room were not abandoned tires.

She peeked, and sure enough, there was a little black sliver, one of the sleepy worms that had fallen from the air vents in the hallway licking at her papery skin with slimy lassitude.

She was dead. She pinched the thing between her fingers and flicked it indiscriminately away from her.

It seemed to bounce off one of the big black things in front of her. They stopped huddling and fought to suck up the morsel.

The note faded.

Sue tried singing but she forgot the words. She knew then she had the intoxicating worm venom in her.

Sue sang.

"Row-row-row your boat," she belted out. The faces on the others told her she was wrong. She half suspected that as he aged, Darren Minor performed with a teleprompter somewhere on stage just out of sight of the crowd. I mean how many songs did this guy write? "I need a teleprompter."

The song went on. A weird one. Sue did not see a top forty hit here. Maybe she started weaving or swaying or tap dancing. One of the Cubans grabbed her.

"Go back to Belgium!" she growled, and in ripping away her arm, stumbled forward toward the center of the room and the hungry things. The next grab was not as gentle, tugging her by the waistband of her shorts and yanking her back until her head clunked against the bulkhead, colliding with a bare rivet head.

When Sue checked the wound, her hand came away bloody.

"Shit," someone groaned.

The mounds of black moved toward her.

"Don't worry," a female voice said. "I got it."

"Ow," Sue whined. "You hurt me."

Knees started to give way, but she was shot straight as the song was obliterated by a powerful buzz. The buzz made the air itch like walking through a mosquito infested jungle trail. The itch grew. Sue lay down and swatted at her ears. Nothing more irritating than trying to sleep with a mosquito buzzing around your ear, little vampires.

Vampires. There were vampires in this room.

Sue cracked her eyes. She was so tired. Most of the room swam, but there was an undeniable field of black closing on her.

"Sue!" the concerned mosquito called.

She was, again, grabbed by the waistband and hoisted to her feet. Then the buzz grew until the subtle growth of hair on her arms stood at attention.

There was a scrawny chicken pecking away at controls of the wall panel with cock-eyed aplomb. Each peck made the buzz more intent.

The nearest collection of black stretched its length to a standing position, and turning, showed its true self. Dropping the lapels of its flowing black cape exposed a long-nosed, eastern European face. Bela Lugosi closed in on Sue.

There was a bang. A gunshot, Gary Cooper shot the thing from across the room, but of course it did not work. The vampire ignored the shot. But there were other vampires and they descended on Cooper and eviscerated him. Other cowboys, seeing the failure of the six shooter, fled. Sue understood. The chicken pecked away. Lugosi, only a few feet away glared into her eyes, holding her with his intense stare. The buzz intensified and added a bass line of thrumming quakes.

Then Lugosi burst, melting a bit, exploding a bit.

Someone drew Sue away from the pool of black that had been Count Dracula.

FOURTEEN

It took some time for the effects of the worm bite to clear from Sue's head. Now, she was clear enough and had a banging headache.

The remainder of the group gathered around the wall panel. Scarface was gone. He had fired the useless shot from his handgun and drew the super eels to him and away from Sue.

Her head hurt. There was no aspirin to be found. Just as well, it would not work well with her coumadin. Then she realized she hadn't taken any of her medications since this thing started, maybe not even the day of discovering Ike. Three days without her medications. She trusted her doctors. She had had a bout of strange dizziness a few years back and the blood thinner had been the preventative to lower the risk of stroke. There were a few other medications too. She trusted Dr. Marko. She would go back on the medications if so instructed (if Marko was still alive). But she remarked on how she felt right now. In pain, tired, but well. She felt well. She felt alive, even while staring death, a horrible death, in the face.

But hadn't she been sitting around Minor Mansions avoiding her gaze from what lay around every corner of that place, death? It was a lovely place, but there were no reprieves from the old folks home save in a box.

Now she faced a death far worse and she, in some bizarre way, felt better than she had in years.

The plan seemed to be coming together. Sue did not join the group. Her curiosity had left her. She was ready to go home. If she could just see her family again, her grandkids, life would be fine. She would never want for anything else again.

But, if all these nuts were right, and her own eyes had confirmed much of the worst, she had to stick it out here in order to protect all the grandkids, all over the world.

These things could get into any water supply.

A lightning flash lit the room through the large, supersonic windows. Sue did not hear the rumble of thunder. Either the windows did the job better than Sue imagined, or they still had some time, a little, before the storm hit and would likely lose all power.

Sonia appeared to be thinking along the same lines. "If we go dark, even for a moment, it could blow the whole thing, make it worse. I have to confess that concentrating the sonic pulses at the pipeline will purge the tube of entities, but it will likely compromise the integrity of the steel composite of the pipe."

"That sounds shaky," Minor said.

"It's a risk," Sonia said, "but it's the best we got." She hit a button on the control board. "Mike, you put in the word to the Consortium?"

A harsh click proceeded the response. "Yeah roger-that," Stewart said. "A Navy clipper will be here by morning with everything we need."

"You don't have all the equipment to stop these things?" Shroom asked. "You just said we have to dig into this right away."

Sonia nodded. "Our end of it." She took off her glasses and gave them a quick wipe on her shirt. "There's still a population of these things in the Earth's crust. We don't know how many, nor how to root them out while they are still down there and wipe out the wasps while still in the nest. Our job is to cap and contain, take all the pressure off the pipe and kill all

the entities within. The Consortium has arranged for the materials to reinforce the pipe and a wildcat crew to come and cap the gusher at the source, keep them contained underground where they have been hiding safely for millions of years."

"And all the loose ones on the rig," Shroom said.

Sonia nodded. "All this," she indicated the suspended speakers, "will be focused on the pipe. The pipe goes down two hundred fathoms and can hold thousands of gallons of crude, or crude contaminated with *Hirt Plattus*."

She gave Sue a weak smile in recognition of the Latin name and its source. Sue returned the look with a small grimace of her own.

"I've got to concentrate on the pipe," Sonia said, "but I can hook you up with a portable version of the guitar bomb, maybe even make it a bit more powerful. I could boost some coms they use to communicate throughout the rig to put out impulses in the right frequency when a sound is introduced into the mic."

Darren Minor slapped the scientist on the back. "If I hear what you're saying, doc," he said, "we gotta take this show on the road and sing for our lives."

"That's exactly what I'm saying."

FIFTEEN

As tired as she was, the apparatus they rigged onto her back felt like chainmail.

Get back to the guitar and Mike Stewart, that was the plan. Until Minor had the Fender strapped on him, he too wore the modified mic apparatus.

The double hatch to lab could slide open automatically after hitting a trigger.

"What shall we sing?" Sue asked as she punched the hatch trigger.

"It's not about melody," Sonia said without turning from her work. "It's about experimenting with amplitude, notes, until you find the right sympathetic frequency."

Sue shrugged as the hatches opened. Their first test was waiting just outside. The biggie that had killed the Major and chased them down the hallway coiled right outside, writhing energetically, hungrily, looking for prey.

"Has a little more pep," Minor said.

Sue tried to swallow in a dry mouth, not sure if she had a note in her desiccated vocal chords.

Shroom started in first, grabbing the shoulder mic and bringing it to his lips. Like all of them, he had a naked speaker cone strapped to his chest.

He started a note, a low, sustained note like a chanter in a pagan temple. Minor joined him with a sweet octave harmony. Sue raised her mic and built on top of the other two chanters' tones. It was awful and difficult to maintain, the croak of the last frog on the pond come October. But she held it and the conjoined noise coming out of the chest speakers seemed stronger for her failure to harmonize with the other men.

The super slug was made aware of their presence by the noise but showed little sign of being able to lock on. It lunged blindly then began rolling on the floor.

The BioFlouretic agent and the other Cuban belted their notes, which, like Sue, were atonal. The sourness of the note almost made Sue cry. She wanted to stop. It was the musical version of sucking on a lemon. And, she was tired. Dead tired. But it was better than just being dead, and she could see the odd singing was working. Sue's throat complained, and she sang on.

The creature danced like sizzling meat on a frying pan. Minor, the consummate jammer, got the idea quickly and started to vary his tones to add to the dissonance rather than make a pretty chord.

The demon worm bubbled and oozed. It leaked and then split, a slug assaulted with salt. It exploded into black bean soup all over the corridor. The group stepped back, checked themselves for eel bits, and then began to laugh with triumph and relief.

"Next," Sue said, "get up under those vents full of the little ones and give em a blast."

And they did, and the little ones dripped out of the overhead vents like the shower from a gusher.

They peeked up the access tube. No more big ones lodged in there. They climbed. They cleared the hallway and regained the auxiliary cafeteria.

Mike Stewart turned from the wall panel as they entered. "About time you got here."

Another lightning flash, this time with accompanying thunder. The wind howled, a wet spatter audible through the hull. The lights flickered. Outside, the last of the day had died away.

From some lower part of the rig a metallic rumble answered the thunder.

"She's started," Stewart said.

***

From their position in the cafeteria, it seemed like a race between Sonia's sonic bombardment of the pipeline and the tropical storm bulldozing up the Gulf. Several times the lights flickered after a bludgeoning from thunder.

"You know we can't stay here," Shroom said, strapping the guitar onto his boss. "We have to sweep the rig. The things out there are only going to get more lively. We'll never make it onto the navy cutter if we let them fully recover."

"Shroom's right," Minor said, tossing off a quick G chord. "It's up to us to make this place safe so the wildcatters can plug up the pipeline sucking the monsters out of the ground."

In his true accent, devoid of Spanish inflection, the remaining Cuban nodded toward Sue while addressing the group. "She stays here. I can no longer stand to see a woman put into danger. Now, it is not necessary."

"I agree," the last of the BioFlouretic agents said.

Sue started to argue. She did not want to go. She wanted to sleep, even if it meant never waking up again. But this wasn't about her. "No," she said. Her throat was sore. She drank water from a coffee mug to try and reinvigorate her voice.

Darren Minor looked down on her with caring, knowing eyes. "I have to agree on this one, Sue," he said. "There's not a need. We can do it. Every minute we're here, those things are getting friskier."

"We all know," Sue said, hoisting her voice amplifier and securing it over her narrow shoulders. "This isn't about us, or about me. And I'll be damned if I am going to die of fear here while I could be out *there*, dying to save the world. And, by-the-way, that includes my children and grandchildren. I'm here, and I have a stake like any of the rest of you."

The men exchanged glances, smiling meekly.

Minor spoke for them. "Alright, Sue," he said. "I suppose you have the right to die like any of us."

"We gotta start with the common room," Shroom said. "That's where the breach occurred. There's bound to be a ton of em out there."

Stewart rigged up the guitar weapon to be portable like the voice amplifiers. Minor gave the common room a blast before they sorted themselves along the walls, hoping to join their sounds together in the middle to affect anything in the room. It would not be the lab, and none of them had advanced degrees in engineering, but it was a plan and it was a start.

Only a few of the mid-sized eels lingered in plain sight, motionless. It was all the ones they couldn't see, hiding in couch cushions and coffee makers and cupboards that Sue truly feared. But as she had learned, these special noisemakers of Sonia's had some penetration.

Minor played a chord, could have even been a minor chord, and the group sang, not trying to match the chord only listening, no, *feeling*, for that moment when the harmonic frequency is struck, sending shivers through Sue's body and making the devil worms dance like spit on a sidewalk in July.

The visible creatures tried to flee, then held motionless as the sympathetic wave grew in strength and galvanized them in place. Hidden creatures emerged, also struggling to escape the sonic attack. The song reached a pitch as rumbles from below and outside acted as timpani accompaniment. Sonia versus the gathering storm.

The foot-long monsters popped and sizzled to soup just as Sue felt all the hairs on her head stand up straight.

Minor hit the last chord with a Pete Townshend windmilling of his strumming arm.

He had a wide smile on his face as though he had just brought to close a second encore at the last show of a long tour, but had breath for one more if the audience screamed loud enough.

"Okay," he said, swiping at a sheen of sweat on his brow. "Now the rest of this dump."

That's when a particularly close bolt of lightning lit the place followed closely by a responding mortar fire of thunder.

The lights went out.

"Don't suppose anyone brought a flashlight?" Shroom asked.

A weak light issued from a position kitty-corner to Sue. "I got this," the last Cuban said. It was his cellphone, glowing weakly across the common area. As Sue's eyes grew accustomed, the light proved to be sufficient to reveal most of the room. "I don't have much power."

"Let's beat a hasty retreat to safe ground," Minor said.

Sue was about to agree when a powerful light from outside the rig shot through the largest portal just behind the Cuban, obliterating the weak light from his cellphone.

A booming voice spoke from inside the light in an angry, Zeusian jumble.

"What?" Sue asked.

"It's the Navy cruiser," Minor said. "They're coming aboard."

"I hope they brought some lights," Shroom said.

They came up from access ladders coiling around the outside decks of the rig. They were reckless and fast and did not want to hear about dangers of killer eels or devil worms. They plugged the cruiser's power system into the rig and lit it up like Christmas. They quickly rounded up the survivors into the common room, and told them the news.

The one with all the bars on his shoulders, standing tall and straight as a redwood, addressed them. "This rig is now the property of the United States Navy. We will evacuate you folks immediately. You will receive your debrief enroute to the mainland for further processing by representatives of the NSA and CIA and CDC and whatever letters the good people occupying Washington can bring down on you. I am Quartermasse, the XO aboard the good ship *Montrose*, and I'd be pleased to answer any questions you have."

Sue sheepishly raised a hand.

"No questions? Good!" Quartermasse bellowed. "Escort these folks aboard their new home."

A not so friendly escort put a determined hand on each of them. Sue watched for a black squiggle to shoot across the room and cut one of them to pieces.

Another seaman dragged Mike Stewart into the room and shoved them into the scree of survivors.

Sue edged up to him. "They get Sonia yet?"

He shook his head. "I warned her of the situation. She said it was okay; she had given the pipe all she could."

"What about the rest of the things on the ship?" Sue asked.

"I said I didn't think you guys had time to sweep the whole rig," Stewart said. "She said she was on it. Expect something loud to…"

The buzzing boom that issued up from the lower decks shook Sue's innards like a fad weight loss belt. Her skull felt like a tuning fork tied to a speaker at a Metallica concert.

She angled the speakers up toward us, Sue realized and then blacked out.

SIXTEEN

Patsy, Sue's youngest, sat heavily on the coral colored, low-backed chair in the sun room. She was big as a house with her third. The other two rascals were running around the stiff lawned backyard of the Mansions.

"Come on, Mom," Patsy said, one hand on the big swell of her stomach. She made the trip down on her own. She had always been the toughest. "There's no reason for it anymore."

"There was reason enough for me to come here in the first place," Sue said.

"Come on, don't do that, Mom," Patsy said.

Outside, Dan, five, and Celia, three, were hooting it up with some ancient playmate, happy to have children in the place. Everyone was happy to have them, even Sue, though she did not want to listen to her daughter's arguments. She wanted Sue to leave Minor Mansions.

"You were the one who found this place. You said it reminded you of your groupie days or whatever."

"I was never a groupie, dear, and maybe I was just preemptively banishing myself. It made me feel like I had a choice in the matter."

"That's just awful, Mom! And you know it's not true. We offered you a place and so did Francine."

"You were the only one who settled enough to support an extended family, the previous generation included. God love your sisters, but they've always had their own ways that had little to do with me."

"They love you, Mom," Patsy said.

"They do," Sue said. "They do, you've just made room for me. But really, sweety, it's not necessary, I really am happy here."

Just then the french doors opening to the back patio split open and allowed the wild creatures inside.

"Who let those in?" Sue cried.

Her grandchildren growled at her, little Dan flinging himself into her arms, almost knocking Sue's new dentures (tops and bottoms), down her throat.

"Easy, Dan!" Patsy scolded.

Sue laughed.

Darren Minor followed the little monsters into the air conditioned confines of the sunroom, closing the French doors on the Florida swelter.

He pinched the front of his polo shirt and pulled it loose from his chest to let some of the sweat escape. He smiled when he saw Sue, taking her hand.

"Make it okay?" Sue asked.

Minor patted her hand. "I've battled tougher creatures." He winked.

Patsy accepted her daughter into her arms, but kept her eyes on Sue. "Mom," she said, the determination clear in her voice. "After the contamination, how can you stay here? I never wanted you to be here, and you are coming back with me."

Sue and Darren exchanged glances. It was how the deaths at Minor Mansions was explained, a contamination from the plant across the street, though no one seemed to be able to clarify what BioFlouretics did.

"I'm fine, darling, really," Sue said.

"Dress it up however you want, Mom," Patsy said, running a brush through an unruly blond mane, the owner of the wild hair crying out. "But living in a place like this. It's..." She stopped and then covered her daughter's ears. "It's just sitting around waiting to die."

Sue smiled. "My life isn't about dying," she said. "It's about living. And, besides, I'm not alone here." She took Darren Minor's hand, who returned the caring grip.

Minor knelt beside Sue. "And, we're not going to be sitting around here," he said. "I got a few dates this Autumn, and your mom is coming with me."

Patsy's eyebrows lifted. "Oh?" she said. "So, you're clearly over the effects of the contamination and ready to live your life as a groupie?"

"Hah," Minor said.

"I told you she'd say that," Sue said.

"Sue is not my groupie," Darren Minor said. "She's my gal and my partner. She's agreed to stay on here to be my eyes and ears when I can't take her with me. The tour buses keep getting smaller as the hair gets grayer. We've been through thick and thin together, and there isn't anyone I trust more to run this place."

Dan, a bright five-year-old, picked up on some of the concern drifting through the room. "Are you alright, Grandma?" he asked, looking up with big blue eyes.

Sue smiled and ran a hand through his wild shock of sandy hair. "I'm just fine my sweet boy," she said. "Just a bad dream or two, but everyone has those. You just tell yourself it's just a dream and turn over and go back to sleep, no biggie."

"Grandma?" Dan asked, sniffing back at the constant drip in his nose. "How do you know when the bad dream is over? I need mommy or daddy to come tell me."

Sue looked down at the spot on the back of her hand, her right hand, the spot she had been itching at for the last few days, certain she saw something dark just under the skin.

Their bite has a mild hallucinatory effect.

"Honey," she said, "all dreams end, even bad ones. You can't go around worrying about dreams. Life is what happens when your eyes are open and the sun is out. Now, go over there, give your mother a big hug and ask her if she would consider naming your new brother, the one in her belly, Daniel."

They had launched out of NAS JRB (Naval Air Station Joint Reserve Base), New Orleans. Rear Admiral Rosenthall's instructions had been clear, mission parameters obvious. This needed to be the end to it. Lieutenant Commander Peterson agreed. They were coming to the end. Quartermasse was the titular team leader on the waves, but the scientist, the one who was as slim as a toothpick and sharp as an axe, really wore the pants on this adventure. Her name was Sonia. She would not let Peterson call her doctor. He was her missions liaison. He was her military voice.

Secretly, Lieutenant Commander Peterson was losing his mind.

"We cleared the rig, armed with weapons provided by the science Consortium," Quartermasse belted out across a com. "A deck-by-deck cross-search yielded no living organisms. We disembarked from the research rig and let her have it with the gamma sweepers. Nothing could have lived through that. Half my men were on body collection and casualty identification. Now we finish the job."

Peterson straightened. "Yes, sir," he said. "Time to get the ball rolling on Woofer."

Operation Woofer essentially was a diverse armada of Coast Guard cutters and naval emergency response vessels arranged in the form of a vast circle, the rim of a huge speaker. A magnetic vibrating drum hovered above the water, suspended between the ships on cable constructed of a special steel composite some twenty yards long. The huge cylinder jiggling with the controlled bob of each ship at the other end of a supporting hoist line.

"And what about eradicating the pocket of infestation in the Earth's crust?" Peterson asked. "How deep does this thing need to penetrate?"

The slim scientist lowered the binoculars she had been using to monitor the positioning of the device. "We have to accept a degree of uncertainty. However, the expected effect will result in a simultaneous destruction of organisms most likely to escape and trap the rest in the resulting crumbling of the upper mantle. It will take them another hundred million years to dig out."

Dig, dig, dig, the word echoed in Peterson's mind. He scratched at the hand again.

They rode out the calm seas aboard the *Mistral*, a British emergency spill response vessel that was mostly open deck and twice the engine power of a navy cruiser.

"Then we might as well get this party started," Peterson said, taking out his scullery gloves and putting them on. He just needed a little longer. The itch was maddening, but they were almost there. Peterson nodded to an ensign on the deck who raised his hand and fired a flare into the sky only marked by high cirrus clouds.

They all watched the red streak etch the sky and then fall in a fiery arch back toward the Gulf. At the moment the red spark died, a horn aboard the Mistral sounded, similar horns sounding from each of the mission vessels.

Peterson bent his shoulder mic to his mouth. "Now!"

An electric hum shot out from the tethering point aboard the *Mistral*--the high powered batteries made for desalinating sea water in disaster prone regions--and down the high tension wire to the magnetic drum bobbing above the water.

Peterson almost failed to get his protective headphones on; the itch beneath his gloves demanding all his attention.

A fierce howl penetrated the stiff Gulf breeze. The crosstalk on the coms was mates begging the pilots of the ships to pull their vessel heavily to the port. The ships were facing in the same direction in a clockwise direction. Peterson knew the call to port was to pull the armada away from the center.

The metal inside each of the ships complained as the giant magnet at the center of their huddle pulled at every inch of steel.

Though very broad and flat in the keel for an open ocean vessel, the *Mistral* listed heavily to the starboard. A signalman riding the tower at the aft fell from his perch. The man overboard signal sounded. Other ships called out similar alarms as the vessels were drawn violently toward the center.

The ring of Gulf water between the ships frothed with activity like a shoal of bait fish driven to the surface by a marlin.

"Yep," Dr. Sonia Revere muttered to Peterson, "just as we thought. Crumbling the mantle surface would let a fresh pocket of organisms loose. This should be containable. Lieutenant, give the order."

Peterson fingered his com. "Attention, attention," he called over the hiss of the sea breeze. "Shake-n-bake; repeat, shake-n-bake."

Seamen of the royal navy went to their utility belts and donned goggles that had been issued to them by the Consortium as advised by the new expert on the entities, Sonia. The men also produced ordinance that would be familiar looking to any of the men that had worked under the Major. Sleek and slender, the guns were aimed down into the froth created by the swirl of as yet unseen creatures. The first confirmed sighting of the beasts is when a handful--completely worked into a frenzy--shot up out of the scrum and landed on one of the British ensigns.

As the boy screamed, the others stayed the course and pulled the triggers of their weapons. A chaotic thrum of pulses vibrated through the hull. The water some twenty feet below, already a choppy mess, erupted into spumes of melting creatures.

Two men were not shooting down into the sea. It was their job to take care of anyone infected by the creatures. They eyed Peterson who nodded his assent. They burned the compromised ensign with flame throwers that were stationed at strategic points on every vessel.

The ensign would understand, Peterson told himself. Peterson, who had been one of those called to the oil rig *Sweetwater* to extract the fallen Major and the smooth rock king from the floating oil extractor that had become the stopper holding the evil in the bottle.

Peterson watched the young man and the super leeches burn to a cinder and itched at his hand.

It was down there, inside him, he knew. He also knew he was losing it. It's what happens when they bite you, get in you. He had reviewed the data, the video logs of activities on the oil rig and had slept little since then.

They had to sweep the rig. It had been their orders.

And they would call him crazy if he told anyone. Of that he was certain, say it was the trauma of being exposed to the events aboard the rig.

But he knew differently. From time-to-time he could see it, the little patch of black where the worm was digging in. Still groggy from the Sonia sonic blasts, the creature just barely evaded Peterson's searching fingernails.

Yes, he was mad. They'd be right about that, but not for the right reasons. They'd tell themselves he talked himself into seeing the dark circle just slip out of view in the spot where he had worn away his flesh to the translucent under skin.

The lieutenant commander kept digging, knowing there was no use in reporting his infection. They'd all know soon enough, and no matter the martial steps taken as part of operation Woofer, there was no escape.

CHECK OUT OTHER GREAT
DEEP SEA THRILLERS

THEY RISE
by Hunter Shea

Some call them ghost sharks, the oldest and strangest looking creatures in the sea.

Marine biologist Brad Whitley has studied chimaera fish all his life. He thought he knew everything about them. He was wrong. Warming ocean temperatures free legions of prehistoric chimaera fish from their methane ice suspended animation. Now, in a corner of the Bermuda Triangle, the ocean waters run red. The 400 million year old massive killing machines know no mercy, destroying everything in their path. It will take Whitley, his climatologist ex-wife and the entire US Navy to stop them in the bloodiest battle ever seen on the high seas.

SERPENTINE
by Barry Napier

Clarkton Lake is a picturesque vacation spot located in rural Virginia, great for fishing, skiing, and wasting summer days away.

But this summer, something is different. When butchered bodies are discovered in the water and along the muddy banks of Clarkton Lake, what starts out as a typical summer on the lake quickly turns into a nightmare.

This summer, something new lives in the lake...something that was born in the darkest depths of the ocean and accidentally brought to these typically peaceful waters.

It's getting bigger, it's getting smarter...and it's always hungry.

CHECK OUT OTHER GREAT DEEP SEA THRILLERS

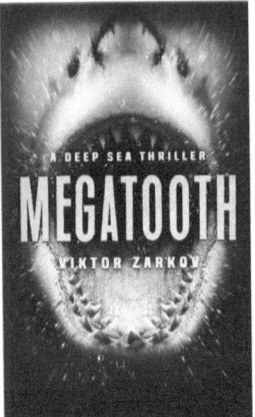

MEGATOOTH
by Viktor Zarkov

When the death rate of sperm whales rises dramatically, a well-respected environmental activist puts together a ragtag team to hit the high seas to investigate the matter. They suspect that the deaths are due to poachers and they are all driven by a need for justice.

Elsewhere, an experimental government vessel is enhancing deep sea mining equipment. They see one of these dead whales up close and personal...and are fairly certain that it wasn't poachers that killed it.

Both of these teams are about to discover that poachers are the least of their worries. There is something hunting the whales...

Something big
Something prehistoric.
Something terrifying.
MEGATOOTH!

BLOOD CRUISE
by Jake Bible

Ben Clow's plans are set. Drop off kids, pick up girlfriend, head to the marina, and hop on best friend's cruiser for a weekend of fun at sea. But Ben's happy plans are about to be changed by a tentacled horror that lurks beneath the waves.

International crime lords! Deep cover black ops agents! A ravenous, bloodsucking monster! A storm of evil and danger conspire to turn Ben Clow's vacation from a fun ocean getaway into a nightmare of a Blood Cruise!

CHECK OUT OTHER GREAT DEEP SEA THRILLERS

LOCH NESS REVENGE
by Hunter Shea

Deep in the murky waters of Loch Ness, the creature known as Nessie has returned. Twins Natalie and Austin McQueen watched in horror as their parents were devoured by the world's most infamous lake monster. Two decades later, it's their turn to hunt the legend. But what lurks in the Loch is not what they expected. Nessie is devouring everything in and around the Loch, and it's not alone. Hell has come to the Scottish Highlands. In a fierce battle between man and monster, the world may never be the same. Praise for THEY RISE : "Outrageous, balls to the wall...made me yearn for 3D glasses and a tub of popcorn, extra butter!" – The Eyes of Madness "A fast-paced, gore-heavy splatter fest of sharksploitation." The Werd "A rocket paced horror story, I enjoyed the hell out of this book." Shotgun Logic Reviews

TERROR FROM THE DEEP
by Alex Laybourne

When deep sea seismic activity cracks open a world hidden for millions of years, terrifying leviathans of the deep are unleashed to rampage off the coast of Mexico. Trapped on an island resort, MMA fighter Troy Deane leads a small group of survivors in the fight of their lives against pre-historic beasts long thought extinct. The terror from the deep has awoken, and it will take everything they have to conquer it.

www.ingramcontent.com/pod-product-compliance
Lightning Source LLC
Chambersburg PA
CBHW051952170626
46808CB00007B/2589